Gilderoy Wells Griffin

Memoir of Col. Chas. S. Todd

Gilderoy Wells Griffin

Memoir of Col. Chas. S. Todd

ISBN/EAN: 9783337092979

Printed in Europe, USA, Canada, Australia, Japan

Cover: Foto ©Andreas Hilbeck / pixelio.de

More available books at **www.hansebooks.com**

BIOGRAPHY

OF

COLONEL CHARLES S. TODD.

MEMOIR

OF

COL. CHAS. S. TODD.

BY

G. W. GRIFFIN,

U. S. CONSUL AT COPENHAGEN,

AUTHOR OF "STUDIES IN LITERATURE," ETC., EIC.

PHILADELPHIA:

CLAXTON, REMSEN & HAFFELFINGER.

1873.

Entered, according to Act of Congress, in the year 1872, by

CLAXTON, REMSEN & HAFFELFINGER,

in the Office of the Librarian of Congress at Washington.

STEREOTYPED BY J. FAGAN & SON, PHILADELPHIA.

PRINTED BY MOORE BROTHERS,

Franklin Buildings, Sixth St., below Arch,

Philadelphia.

Dedication.

TO

THE HON. JOHN SCOTT HARRISON

THIS VOLUME IS DEDICATED, AT THE
EXPRESSED WISH OF HIS FATHER'S
EARLY FRIEND, WHOSE LIFE
AND HISTORY ARE RE-
CORDED IN IT.

I N the publication of this volume, I can but feel that the people of Kentucky, and of the West, will take some degree of interest in the perusal of a work devoted to the life and public services of one who played such a prominent part in the history of the times in which he lived.

Since this volume was ready for the press, I found, among some papers left at my disposal by Colonel Todd a short time before his death, a manuscript copy of a lecture he delivered in 1849, at Frankfort, Ky., on " Russia, her Resources, Religion, Literature, &c." Colonel Todd's residence in Russia, in the capacity of United States Minister to that country, his fine classical education and taste in literature, gave him many advantages for the investigation of the history and resources of that semi-barbarous nation about which so little is known even to this day. I have, for these reasons, thought best to print the lecture entire in this memoir.

I have also embraced in this work, to the exclusion of much matter of my own, a number of Colonel Todd's speeches and state papers; and also some extended extracts from a work entitled " Sketches of the Civil and

Military Services of William Henry Harrison," by Colonel
Todd and Mr. Benjamin Drake. This book is now out
of print; but it had in its day a very large sale. It was
published by G. P. James, of Cincinnati, Ohio, in 1840.
More than twenty thousand copies were sold, and as
many more were distributed, in pamphlet form, throughout the country as a campaign document.

Colonel Todd, on one occasion, pointed out to me such
passages of the book as were written by himself, and
those written by Mr. Drake.

Colonel Todd, as many of my readers doubtless know,
bore a very prominent part in the election of Harrison,
which was perhaps the most exciting Presidential canvass
in the history of the country.

Many a story have I heard, when a boy, from the lips
of my dear and venerated grandfather, of that interesting
epoch, so familiarly known as the Log Cabin or Hard
Cider Campaign. My grandfather was a very zealous
Democrat, and he used to tell me how much the enthusiasm of the Whigs annoyed him at that time. " For once,
and only once," he said, " in the history of our country, did
the Whig speeches, and barbecues, and banners, and transparencies, and cannon, strike terror into the hearts of the
Unterrified."

I remember his telling me, on one occasion, of some
of the most enthusiastic Harrison men carrying, in the
midst of a great parade through the streets of Louisville,
an immense log cabin on their shoulders, the weight of
which would have been enough to crush them to death,
had it not been for their enthusiasm and the shouts of
thousands of people enlivening their march.

In one of these parades, Jim Porter, the great Kentucky

giant, who was by far the tallest man in all the world, appeared, wearing a large coon-skin cap, and dressed in a hunter's uniform made of deer-skin and trimmed with bright-colored fringe. He swung his great rifle, which was over eight feet long, across his huge shoulders, and excited the utmost delight and astonishment wherever he went.

Some years afterward, I went to see the great giant at Shippingport, a little town a few miles below Louisville, where he then resided. I expressed to him my deep regret at not having been able to see him in that famous parade, when he very kindly opened a wardrobe, and donned his coon-skin cap and gay uniform-coat. He presented a magnificent picture to my boyish sight, before which all my wildest dreams about giants paled into utter insignificance, and even to-day I think of that interview with no ordinary satisfaction and delight. "Those were great times," said the giant, "that we had in the Hard-Cider Campaign. We shall not see the like again." And indeed, judging from all that I have heard in regard to that memorable canvass, few, I think, will be inclined to disagree with him.

I could relate many such incidents, interesting enough, doubtless, in their way; but I have preferred to give in the following pages the more solid facts of history, and I have given them as well as I could.

2

CHAPTER I.

CHAPTER II.

CHAPTER III.

CHAPTER IV.

CHAPTER V.

CHAPTER VI.

CHAPTER VII.

BIOGRAPHY

OF

COLONEL CHARLES S. TODD.

CHAPTER I.

The Author's first Acquaintance with Colonel Todd — Characteristics of
Colonel Todd as a Writer and a Man.

I DID not become personally acquainted with the
distinguished soldier and statesman who forms
the subject of this memoir until the spring of 1867.
We had, however, been associated some time previously in the editorial management of the Louisville
Industrial and Commercial Gazette. At that time he
resided in Owensboro, Kentucky, where he prepared
no inconsiderable portion of the editorial matter for
the paper. He was a quick and fluent writer, and
almost every mail was sure to bring something from
his pen. I was forcibly struck by the readiness with
which he comprehended all the plans of the paper,
and by the spirit and determination with which he
entered into them. It seemed that the slightest hint
from the publisher that an article was desired upon
any subject was all that was necessary to have him
produce it in the most complete and satisfactory

18

manner. He displayed a knowledge of every subject upon which he wrote that was really extraordinary. He seemed to have a high and a noble purpose
in everything that he undertook. He had been all
his life a very active and energetic man. He was a
highly accomplished classical scholar. He scorned
to make a show of knowledge which he did not possess. He was a thorough hater of all shams and
conceits. All the best attributes of humanity were
centred in him. There was not a particle of selfish-
ness in his nature. There was no ostentation about
him. He possessed dignity without haughtiness, and
a courage which no mortal man could overcome. He
was of a very kind disposition. He seemed to have
lived always in an interchange of the gentlest offices.
He never allowed trifles to fret and annoy him. He
was in every respect a perfect model of a Christian
gentleman. He could not do a mean or a little act.
No weeds of bitterness ever grew in his manly
bosom. He was a good man, a true man, and a
brave man. I shall never forget the first time I saw
him. I was busy one morning writing at my desk
upon a subject that I knew very little about. I could
not write a single line that seemed to me to have any
sense in it. My poor brain was taxed almost beyond
endurance, and I was about to give up in despair,
when I happened to cast my eyes toward the door,
and saw a fine-looking, elderly gentleman, with the
kindliest face in the world, advancing toward me.
He seemed to understand, as if by intuition, the
nature of my trouble, and I immediately rose to
speak to him and tell him my name and ask his in
return. He did not give me an opportunity, but

took me by both hands, and said, "If I judge cor-
rectly, you are my editorial associate." I bowed an
assent, when he said, "I have often helped you before, my young friend, and I beg the pleasure of being allowed to do so again." He immediately sat
down at my desk, and, after looking at my article,
which was entitled, "The Duty of the Government to
repair the Levees of the Mississippi," he smiled
pleasantly, tore off the heading and pasted it on
another slip of paper, and wrote, in about ten or
fifteen minutes, one of the best articles ever written
upon this subject. It is scarcely necessary for me
to say that I was grateful for the kindness of my benefactor, and tried to make known to him my gratitude in the best way I could. He rose from his seat,
and, again taking me by both hands, said, "It is in
our power to be of much help to one another. You
have youth, and I experience, which, perhaps, next
to an unsullied conscience, is the most valuable thing
in this life." He did not part from me without giving me a very cordial invitation to visit him at the
residence of his son, Mr. Isaac Shelby Todd, where
he said he would remain for several weeks, and
would expect me every day until I called.

Such was the beginning of one of the most charming acquaintances of my life, and I record with no
little satisfaction that from that time up to the day
of his death the warmest feelings of personal friendship existed between us.

When he died I lost one of the best and truest
friends I ever had. I shall not see his like again in
this world, but the memory of his love and unremitting kindness will ever be to me a pleasure inesti-

mable.   In endeavoring to give some account of his life and public services, I shall not attempt anything like a panegyric or eulogy upon his character, but will try to relate faithfully and conscientiously some important incidents in the history of Kentucky and of the nation, and to describe, in a plain, truthful, and straightforward manner, the characteristics of a man who for more than half a century was felt to be a power in the land, and who was loved, honored, and respected by all who knew him.

CHAPTER II.

Birth and Parentage of Colonel Todd — Sketch of his Father, Judge Thomas Todd — Education of Young Todd.

CHARLES STEWART TODD was born on the 22d of January, 1791, between Danville and Stanford, Kentucky, in the old county of Lincoln. At the time of his birth, the State was not a member of the confederacy.   It was in what is called the transition period, but was passing rapidly from the pioneer stage to the dignity of an established and well-regulated commonwealth.   The Hon. Thomas Todd, the father of the subject of this sketch, was one of the most eminent men in the nation.   He immigrated to Kentucky from Virginia when about twenty years of age.   He chose the profession of the law, and devoted himself so earnestly to its duties that he soon became known as one of the ablest lawyers in the Western country.   The honors of his profession came thick and rapidly upon him. His counsel was sought not only at home but abroad. He rose to the position of chief justice, the highest judicial office of the State. It is said that his means were so limited that he studied his profession by fire-light.

Some idea of his ability can be formed from the marvellous facility with which he comprehended the difficulties of the celebrated Land Law of Virginia of 1779. In the passage of this law, the legislative authorities neglected to provide for a general survey of the State, but authorized every owner of a land-warrant to make his own entry and survey. The owner, of course, located his land-warrant wherever he chose, but was required to do so in such a way that a subsequent locater could enter the adjoining land. The system of registration under no circumstances could have been more defective. It was with the greatest difficulty that a title could be established at all. As a natural consequence, interminable disputes and litigation followed.

The ingenuity and talent of the greatest lawyers in America were called into requisition. No one, however, achieved a greater reputation in the adjustment of these perplexing difficulties than Judge Todd. His success was such that President Jefferson, in 1807, called him to a seat on the Supreme Federal Bench. He held this position until his death. His friend and associate, Justice Story, pronounced the following tribute to his memory: "Mr. Justice Todd possessed many qualities admirably fitted for the proper discharge of judicial functions. He had uncommon patience and candor in investi-

3

gation ; great clearness and sagacity of judgment; a
cautious but steady energy ; a well-balanced independence ; a just respect for authority, and, at the same
time, an unflinching adherence to his own deliberate
opinions of the law.   His modesty imparted a grace
to an integrity and singleness of heart which won
for him the general confidence of all who knew him.
He was not ambitious of innovations upon the settled principles of the law, but was content with the
more unostentatious character of walking in the
trodden paths of jurisprudence — '*super antiquas
vias legis.*' From his diffident and retiring habits, it
required a long acquaintance with him justly to appreciate his judicial as well as his personal merits.
His learning was of a useful and solid cast; not,
perhaps, as various or as comprehensive as that of
some men, but accurate and transparent, and appli-
cable to the daily purposes of the business of human
life.   In his knowledge of the local law of Kentucky
he was excelled by few, and his brethren drew
largely upon his resources to administer that law, in
the numerous cases which then crowded the docket
of the Supreme Court from that judicial circuit; what
he did not know he never affected to possess, but
sedulously sought to acquire.   He was content to
learn without assuming to dogmatize.   Hence he
listened to an argument for the purpose of instruction and securing examination, and not merely for
that of confutation or debate.   Among his associates
he enjoyed an enviable respect, which was constantly
increasing as he became more familiarly known to
them.   His death was deemed by them a great
public calamity, and in the memory of those who

survive him his name has ever been cherished with a warm and affectionate remembrance. No man ever clung to the Constitution of the United States with a more strong and resolute attachment. And in the grave cases which were agitated in the Supreme Court of the United States during his judicial life, he steadfastly supported the constitutional doctrines which Mr. Chief Justice Marshall promulgated in the name of the Court. It is to his honor, and it should be spoken, that, though bred in a different political school from that of the Chief Justice, he never failed to sustain those great principles of constitutional law on which the security of the Union depends. He never gave up to party what he thought belonged to the country. For some years before his death he was sensible that his health was declining, and that he might soon leave the bench, to whose true honor and support he had been so long and zealously devoted. To one of his brethren, who had the satisfaction of possessing his unreserved confidence, he often communicated his earnest hope that Mr. Justice Trimble might be his successor, and he bore a willing testimony to the extraordinary ability of that eminent judge. It affords a striking proof of his sagacity and foresight; and the event fully justified the wisdom of his choice. Although Mr. Justice Trimble occupied his station on the bench of the Supreme Court for a brief period only, yet he has left on the records of the Court enduring monuments of talents and learning fully adequate to all the exigencies of the judicial office. To both of these distinguished men, under such circumstances, we may well apply the touching panegyric of the poet:

'Fortunati ambo ;
Nulla dies unquam memori vos eximet avo.' ''

Judge Todd gave every attention to the education of his son. He encouraged him to cultivate a taste not only for the classics but for almost every species of knowledge.

Young Todd was placed at an early age at the Transylvania Seminary at Lexington, Kentucky, for the purpose of preparing for a more thorough course of study at the celebrated college of William and Mary in Virginia. He graduated at this last-named institution of learning in 1809.

About a year afterward he went to Litchfield, Conn., to attend a course of law lectures by Judges Reeves and Gould. At Litchfield he pursued his studies with the utmost energy. He was licensed to practise law in 1811, and opened an office in the following year at Lexington, Ky.; but at that time the second war with Great Britain broke out, and he determined to take part in the contest.

CHAPTER III.

War of 1812 — Young Todd volunteers and is rapidly Promoted — His
Gallantry — Battle of the Thames — McArthur's Expedition — Todd's
distinguished Services.

THE spirit of war was nowhere more brilliantly
illustrated than in Kentucky. The whole
State, from the Big Sandy to the Mississippi, was
alive, as it were, with restless energy and activity.
In the mean time Hull's surrender was announced.
It served only to add fuel to the flame. Hull was
at once proclaimed a traitor. No language was sufficiently strong to express the detestation in which
he was held. The Kentucky troops were impatient
to be led to the scene of action, but they moved
amid the most distressing circumstances. They
were indifferently armed and wretchedly clothed.
They suffered privations almost unheard of. The
country to be crossed was but a succession of
swamps and marshes. The Secretary of War was
unable to supply means of transportation. Notwithstanding these obstacles, the ardor and enthusiasm
of the volunteers remained unabated.

William Henry Harrison, on whom the President
had conferred the rank of Major-General, assumed
command of the forces in the West. Harrison was
an especial favorite with the Kentucky troops, and
his appointment served to increase their enthusiasm.

Young Todd was among the first to volunteer his
services, and he was elected ensign in one of the
Lexington companies, but was soon afterward ap-

pointed to a position in the Quartermaster-General's Department. He was afterward assigned to another position, and was soon actively engaged against the enemy. We learn from McAfee's History of the War of 1812, and from Hall's Life of Harrison, that in the campaign which followed Colonel Todd rendered invaluable service.

General Harrison, in a letter to the War Department, recommended him for a captaincy in the line, saying that "he appeared to combine the ardor of youth with the maturity of age."

The campaign terminated in the unfortunate battle of the River Raisin. The movement to that point was made by General Winchester. It was made in violation of Harrison's instructions in regard to the campaign. Harrison's instructions were conveyed by the subject of my sketch from the right wing to the left of the army, a distance of one hundred miles, through a swampy wilderness. McAfee, in his History of the War of 1812, says that "Colonel Todd performed the hazardous journey with a secrecy and dispatch highly creditable to his enterprise." The defeat of Winchester was the defeat of the campaign, but measures were taken to obtain command of the lake prior to active operations in the next campaign. In the mean time the British General Proctor attempted to take Camp Meigs on the Maumee, and Fort Stevenson on the Sandusky, but both attempts were signal failures.

Harrison made a requisition upon the Governor of Kentucky for troops to act in the decisive operations of the campaign. The Governor, the noble and gallant Shelby, around whose peerless name so

many bright and glorious recollections cluster, offered
to lead the troops in person. Four thousand
mounted men rallied on thirty days' notice. The
venerable Governor reached the scene of operations
just as Perry had obtained command of the lake.
The genius of Harrison now shone out in the fulness
of its splendor. He had entire command of the
lake, and was ready at any moment to attack Detroit and Malden. The British forces became
alarmed at the condition of affairs, and began to retreat. Their Indian allies fast deserted them. Less
than one half remained faithful in adversity. Even
the gallant Tecumseh refused to share the fortunes of
Proctor, except on condition that the first favorable
ground should be selected for battle.

The division of Major-General Desha was formed
at right angles, which caused it to face the Indian
line. But, just as the order to advance was about to
be given to Trotter's brigade of Henning's division,
information was obtained through Colonel Wood, of
the Engineers, that the enemy was formed in open
order. This information decided Harrison to charge
the British line with Colonel Johnson's regiment.
Harrison placed himself at the head of the right battalion of this regiment. The enemy was unable to
resist the charge, and gave way in the wildest confusion. The Indians fought with the utmost desperation; but, Tecumseh being killed, they were driven
from every position they assumed.

Colonel Todd was engaged in the battle from the
beginning to the close. He was by the side of Harrison in the charge upon the British regulars, and
was despatched with orders to Governor Shelby,

whose command was stationed at the intersection of the two divisions. Colonel Todd, with this portion of the army, now participated in the action against the Indians, but when the Indians were driven from their position he was recalled to engage in the pursuit of Proctor. In this pursuit Colonel Todd was accompanied by Colonel Wood, Major Payne, Major Chambers, and Captain Langham. There is scarcely an historian, who has given an account of this engagement, but makes some honorable mention of these gallant and accomplished soldiers. The pursuing force, though unable to overtake Proctor, succeeded in capturing his sword, carriage, and papers. Wood and Todd were far in advance of the other officers. The pursuing party succeeded in capturing quite a number of prisoners. A mounted British officer, who was among the captured, endeavored treacherously to shoot Colonel Todd. This attempt was instantly discovered by Captain Wood, who struck the coward down with his sword. Captain Wood was breveted major for gallant conduct in defence of Fort Meigs, lieutenant-colonel for conspicuous service at the battle of Lundy's Lane, and colonel for his heroic part in the defence of Fort Erie. He would have been made brigadier-general of the *elite* of the army had he not fallen in the sortie from the Fort on the 17th of September, 1814. He was wounded in the thigh, and was bayoneted while tendering his sword.

That our readers may form some idea of the importance of the victory on the Thames, we give the following extract from an article entitled "The Military Genius of Harrison," from the pen of Colonel Todd, first printed in 1840, in the Cincinnati *Republican:*

"The strong position of the enemy rendered it probable, that, if the American army should be victorious, the result would be achieved by the loss of many gallant men.

"The British troops occupied the left of the allied army, resting upon an unfavorable view, with its right extending into swamps filled with Indians under Tecumseh.   To undertake to turn the Indians' right would have been hazardous, and certainly attended with great loss of life.   The British line was then properly regarded as the weakest point of the enemy.   In the first instance the charge was intended to be made by the infantry, the front of which was commanded by Trotter; but the fortunately discovered error committed by Proctor in opening his files led to the brilliant conception of charging with the mounted troops of Colonel Johnson.   The result is known to the world, — an entire British army captured and two thousand Indians defeated, with an immense loss of life, by less than fifteen hundred Americans, whose loss was less than thirty killed and forty wounded; and an end put to the war in the Northwest, an important territory restored to the United States, and the uppermost part of Canada conquered.   Other generals have acquired renown by great bloodshed, but in the career of Harrison we recognize equal glory in the results, with much greater prudence and humanity in the preservation of the lives of his patriotic soldiers."

In the fall of 1814, General McArthur undertook an expedition into Canada.   Colonel Todd, having been previously appointed Assistant Inspector-General, acted as McArthur's Adjutant-General.   It was

4

one of the most brilliant and successful expeditions of the war. It was organized at Urbana, and marched from Detroit. It consisted of seven hundred mounted men. Its object was to prevent the enemy from molesting Michigan.

Headley, in his "Second War with England," says: "It was, however, no holiday march. Expedition was necessary for success. The horses were kept to the top of their endurance — straining up acclivities, floundering through swamps, struggling with the rapid current of rivers. This detachment succeeded in penetrating more than two hundred miles into the enemy's country, and to within twenty-five miles of Burlington Height. It marched more than four hundred miles, one hundred and eighty of it through an unbroken wilderness, defeated five hundred militia strongly posted, killed and wounded twenty-seven men, took one hundred and eleven prisoners, and returned with a loss of but one man. McArthur showed himself a skilful and able commander, while *his subordinates deserved the highest commendation.*"

McAfee, in speaking of this expedition, says (see McAfee's History of the War of 1812, page 453): "And thus terminated an expedition which was not surpassed during the war in the boldness of its design and the address with which it was conducted. It was attended with the loss of one man only on our part, while that of the enemy was considerable in men, as well as the injury done to his resources. It was with great difficulty that General Drummond could subsist his troops, with the aid of all the mills in his vicinity, and without them his difficulties must have been greatly increased. General McArthur,

who conceived and conducted the expedition, displayed great bravery and military skill. No one
could have managed his resources with more prudence and effect. His officers and men were also
entitled to the highest praise and gratitude of the
country for their firmness in danger, and the cheerfulness and fortitude with which they obeyed his
orders and endured the greatest hardships."

Major Todd was particularly distinguished. " I
have the support of all the troops," says General
McArthur, "in assuring you that to the military skill,
activity, and intelligence of Major Todd, who acted
as my Adjutant-General, much of the fortunate progress and issue of this expedition is attributable, and
I cheerfully embrace this occasion to acknowledge
the important services which he has at all times rendered me whilst in command of the district. His
various merits justly entitle him to the notice of the
Government."

The following spring Colonel Todd was promoted
to the position of Inspector-General of the district.

CHAPTER IV.

Colonel Todd resumes the Practice of the Law at Frankfort — Becomes interested in Masonry — His Address before Mt. Horan Lodge — He is married to Miss Shelby.

AT the close of the war, Colonel Todd returned to Frankfort, Ky., and resumed the practice of the law. He soon became regarded as one of the foremost men at the bar.

At this time he became very much interested in the study of Masonry. He delivered a number of addresses on this subject that attracted a good deal of attention. The following address he delivered before the Mt. Horan Lodge, at Frankfort, June 24th, 1815. It displays in an able and learned manner the precepts of this noble brotherhood: .

Worshipful Master, Officers, and Brethren : — Meeting on the *level* of equal privileges, social feelings, and humble hearts, let us endeavor, in a concise manner, to do justice to the purpose for which we are convened this day — the celebration of the anniversary of a distinguished patron of Freemasonry, St. John the Baptist. The attempt, it is hoped, will be received with that *charity* which forms a main pillar in our ancient edifice ; and, whilst "the imperfections of a brother claim a brother's indulgence," you will bear with me in an unadorned exposition of some of the fundamental principles of our Order.

Masonry, if not coeval with mankind, originated with the *fall* of man, and with the wants which that fall produced. It has, therefore, been justly asserted, that the causes more immediately contributing to the introduction of the art may be traced to the period of the first sin, since, in the desire to afford a covering and protection to Eve, Adam resorted to suitable contrivances, which, upon gradual improvement, became the foundation of *operative* Masonry. Thus in its early origin do we recognize that special regard to the fair sex which characterizes all true and faithful Masons ; and if the most lovely part of creation be denied the beauties of the Mystic Order, a satisfactory apology may be found in the consideration that *their own* feelings, open as day to melting charity, prompt them to offer balsam to the wounded spirit, and their "own hearts are the *Lodges* in which virtue presides."

Man in the pristine ages of barbarism was too fatally inclined to regard as his enemy that fellow-being whom the Creator in his wisdom had destined to become the participator of his blessings. Consequently, at different periods of the world, Masonry was suffered to decline ; but, founded as it is on the eternal rock of truth and brotherly love, it withstood the shocks of superstition and prejudice, and, in proportion to the progress of science and civilization, its pillars were strengthened, and further knowledge disclosed new beauties. The introduction of the Christian Religion, the revival of letters, and the doctrines of Masonry, each operating upon the hopes, the understanding, and the heart of man, gradually directed his efforts to the purposes of civilization ; and under their influence it was happily found, that, renouncing the contracted views of the selfish in order to embrace the more enlivening qualities of the social principle, he threw off the fetters of national animosity, and became himself the ardent advocate for the amelioration of his species.

In the history of the character and progress of Masonry, we can boast among its members and patrons the most distinguished men of every age. Cæsar, Alfred, and the most illustrious monarchs of the British Empire deigned to descend to the *level* of a brother, and participated in all the rites and blessings of the institution. The most pious of divines, the most moral of moralists, the most renowned of

warriors, the most zealous of patriots, and the most enlightened of every art and of every science, have been classed
among the members of an institution which embraces the
noblest feelings and the most liberal principles — whose
canopy is Heaven! and whose usefulness is commensurate
with creation!

The first corner-stone in Masonry is a belief in the Eternal God, the Grand Architect of the Universe. With this
foundation, can its tendency be presumed to be either irre-
ligious, immoral, or disorganizing? Yet in every age attempts have been made to inculcate such doctrines; and,
even at this day, the horrors of the Inquisition have extended to the persecution of the meek and humble tenets
of brotherly love. In regard to the secrecy with which our
proceedings are conducted, it may be proper to remark that
benefits which are common and easily procured are but
slightly appreciated. It is the veneration created by im-
penetrable mystery, added to the usefulness and moral
worth which ought to distinguish Masons, that has preserved it unimpaired through the lapse of ages; for "Masonry is not only the most ancient, but the most moral institution that ever subsisted. Every character, figure, and
emblem depicted in a Lodge, has a moral tendency, and
inculcates the practice of virtue."

Upon entering the Lodge, we *divest* ourselves, as far as
practicable, of all the follies, the vanities, the petty ambition, the vexation, and the turmoil to which an intercourse
with the world necessarily exposes us. In the bosom of the
Lodge, private animosity, family jealousy, political bicker-
ings, and religious altercation are forgotten; and, in the language of our excellent Constitution, we may say that "freedom of opinion thus indulged, but its points never discussed,
is the happy influence under which the unity of this honorable society has been preserved from time immemorial —
upon which account Masonry has become the centre of
union, and the means of conciliating among those that
might otherwise have remained at a perpetual distance,

causing them to love as brethren and heirs of the same hope, partaking of the same promises, children of the same God, and candidates for the same Heaven." And, again, "Masons, being declared of the oldest religion, universally acknowledged as such, and of all nations, are bound to live upon the *square, level,* and *plumb* with each other, following the footsteps of their predecessors in cultivating the peace and harmony of the Lodge, without distinction of sect or political party."

Upon the subject of the *abuses* of Masonry, it is important that we should seriously reflect. Let us convince the world, by our conduct, whilst *out* of the Lodge, of the excellence of the principles inculcated *in it.* The institution is holy and enlightened! Let not the world, therefore, withdraw its regard because some of our professors are unworthy. It behooves us, by the correctness of our conduct, to rebut an imputation so dishonorable. That some of us do not act conformably to the principles of our Order is not conclusive evidence that those principles are in themselves improper. As well might the enemies of Masonry deny us in this world the comforts of the religion of the meek and humble Jesus, and the hopes that religion encourages of life everlasting, because we know that some of its professors are found unworthy of the high trust committed to them. Let us, then, cherish a strict regard to truth and brotherly love. Let us regulate our conduct according to the golden rule of "doing unto all men as we would that all men should do unto us." Let us cultivate peace and harmony with our fellow-creatures; gently reprove the foibles of each other; extend to the distressed, either of mind or body, the hand of diffusive charity; and, above all, like the Great Architect of the Universe, let us judge a brother in mercy.

When the best men, and the most distinguished patriots — when such men as Washington, Franklin, and Warren have condescended to *labor* with us in the same vineyard, ought we not to be doubly excited to honorable exertion in the path of rectitude? Respect for the constituted authorities is a fundamental pillar of the Order. Let us, then, by a just sense of patriotism, convince our country that we are worthy of the glorious inheritance purchased by the blood of our fathers. Let us show that, by a temporary retirement from worldly commerce into the bosom of the Lodge and the " All-seeing Eye," we may, from the reception of virtuous · precepts, return again with better capacities to discharge our duty as citizens. In becoming Masons we do not cease to be men, because whilst nature exists the passions and the frailties incident to that nature will also continue. No civil, no moral institution can totally eradicate the sin inseparably connected with our existence. To correct its tendency has been the principal design in all societies. So, in Masonry, we do not entirely cease to feel all those dangerous passions which not unfrequently set a troubled world in motion. To calm the impetuous dispositions of the heart, " to *square* our actions by the rules of rectitude, persevere in the *rule* of our duty, and restrain our passions within the *compass* of propriety," are among the benign principles of our Order; and thrice happy is he who, prac- tising them, can say : This institution and these things have made me a better man, and a more useful citizen.

Among the causes which have tended, at various periods of the world, to excite temporary prejudice against the nature and effects of Masonry, the character and deport- ment of its members whilst *out* of the Lodge may be deemed most serious. It is, as it ought to be, the touch- stone of our creed. Those *without* can only appreciate the principles taught *within* by an attentive observance of our conduct as men and as citizens. Let us, then, my brethren, by a discreet, honorable, and virtuous career, study to evince our attachment to the landmarks of the Order, and thereby command the confidence of the world in their beneficial tendency and effect. We cannot presume to be exempt from those evils that are necessarily attendant upon human- ity. Let us, however, reclaim, as far as practicable, the frailties of our nature. Let us cultivate the social virtues —

zealously regard the qualities of prudence, temperance, and of a meek demeanor. And, finally, let us show to the world, that, in becoming *Masons*, we become better *men*.

In regard to those who may hereafter solicit the benefits of our institution, let us be particularly careful to embrace none whose honorable principles and whose correct deportment do not guarantee an observance of the admirable tenets of Masonry. A disregard of this principle has, in every instance, procured for the craft temporary unpopularity. Let us, as far as possible, repair the breach, and in future let none enter who are not worthy of the high estate. Let us at all times trust in our Leader, the Grand Architect of the Universe. Let us, by due *preparation*, be the better enabled to *pass* through the *trials* we may have to encounter. Let us, by *prudence* and *caution*, avoid the dangers that surround us in the *rugged path of life*, that, when "removed from this *terrestrial* Lodge, we may be admitted, by the *password of grace*, into the *Lodge celestial*, to an everlasting *refreshment* within the *vail*." Finally, my brethen, by "*faith* in God, *hope* in immortality, and *charity* to all mankind," may we ascend, by the *ladder* of honorable exertion, to that Lodge which is the residence of "the spirits of just men made perfect," and governed by the Grand Master of the Universe, whose *Tyler* is death, and whose *portal* the grave!

In 1816, Colonel Todd was married to Letitia Shelby, the youngest daughter of Governor Shelby. She was one of the most beautiful and gifted women in the State. Her features were regular and classical, and her complexion was of the most dazzling whiteness. No one could be in her presence without being impressed with her beauty and accomplishments. I have seen a portrait of her by Jouett, one of the finest artists in the country. It is indeed a splendid specimen of art, and is regarded as a per-

5

fect likeness; but I am satisfied that no art could do justice to the beauty that took all hearts captive.

Colonel Todd first saw her at Frankfort, Ky., the capital of the State, and was at once deeply impressed with her charms. She was surrounded by a gay and brilliant circle, but her eyes were fixed on him alone. It was with both a clear case of love at first sight.

"At first sight they changed eyes."

Colonel Todd was then an officer in the regular army, and was compelled to join his regiment. After standing the separation as long as he could, he applied for a furlough. This being denied him, he addressed Miss Shelby in an open letter enclosed to her father. Governor Shelby saw proper to withhold the letter. It was, however, accidentally discovered by her, and, after reading it, she evinced such attachment for her lover that the most cordial consent was given to their union.

Colonel Todd lived very happily with his wife until her death, which occurred the 22d of July, 1868.

CHAPTER V.

Colonel Todd is appointed Secretary of State — His Election to the Legislature over Judge Marshall and Judge Bibb — His Re-election over General Hardin — Is appointed Minister to Bogota — His Discharge of his Mission approved by John Q. Adams — He returns to the United States, and Settles on a Farm in Shelby County, Kentucky — His Intelligence and Enterprise as a Farmer — His Services to Agriculture.

IN the fall of 1816, Colonel Todd was appointed Secretary of State by Governor Madison. On the death of Madison, Colonel Todd resigned his position, as it was expected that the incoming administration would be under the control of a different political policy.

In 1817, Colonel Todd was elected to the legislature of Kentucky, after a very exciting and hotly contested canvass. There were two candidates opposed to him, Judge Marshall and Judge Bibb. Both of these men had great popularity in the district; but Colonel Todd came out triumphant. In 1818 he was again elected, and this time over General Hardin, one of the ablest men in the State.

In 1820, Colonel Todd was appointed minister to Colombia, South America, for the purpose of completing negotiations which had been suspended by the death of Commodore Perry, and to remain as a confidential agent with the pay of a *charge d'affaires.* He was permitted to return to the United States in 1821. He elicited from the administration, during this mission, the highest commendation. The following is a copy of a letter to Colonel Todd from John

Quincy Adams, who was then Secretary of State. The original letter is in possession of L. J. Cist, the distinguished autographic collector of St. Louis:

DEPARTMENT OF STATE, WASHINGTON, 19th July, 1821.

COLONEL CHARLES TODD, Frankfort, Ky.

SIR: Your despatches and letters, with their enclosures, during your absence from the United States, and since your return until your letter of the 20th ultimo, have been duly received at the Department.

I am directed by the President U. S. to express to you his approbation of your conduct during your agency, and his regret that the state of your health prevented you from proceeding to your ultimate destination; and to add his wish that, as soon as your health shall have been restored, so that it may suit your convenience to resume your duties, you would again proceed to the post of your destination.

Your compensation will recommence from the time of your leaving home to repair to that post. You will take such course for proceeding to the Southern continent, as you shall judge most advisable and most convenient to yourself. No particular addition to the instructions heretofore given you is believed to be necessary.

I am, with great respect, Sir,

Your very humble and obedient servant,

(Signed)   JOHN QUINCY ADAMS.

In 1822 he was sent out, in a frigate, with the recognition of the independence of Colombia. The subjoined despatch, sent from Bogota the 4th of July, 1823, to the State Department at Washington, will give the reader some idea of the ability and fidelity with which he discharged the duties assigned him at Bogota.

BOGOTA, 4th July, 1823.

SIR: I have the honor, by a safe private conveyance, of enclosing a duplicate of Nos. 50, 51, 52, 53, and 54; together with their enclosures. You will receive herewith a copy, also, of the statement communicated on the 16th ultimo to General Santander, with the report made by the Judge of the Supreme Court of the Conference already referred to. I submit, at the same time, a copy of what I supposed to be the substance of that conversation, that you may be possessed of every circumstance connected with that unpleasant alternative. Among the documents delivered to General Santander, was a translation of so much of the messages of the President of the United States in 1811, 1817, 1818, 1819, and 1820, as referred to the South American contest, and the views and acts of the Government growing out of its progress; a translation of the confidential conversation with the President in September, 1821, the substance of which has been already communicated to you; and a translation of so much of the Instructions to Commodore Perry as contains an account of the efforts of the Government by negotiation in favor of the South American Cause, and of the reasons recommending the propriety and advantages of the neutral policy of the United States.

The admission made by the Vice-President of his entertaining the same impression which other persons in authority had candidly acknowledged with respect to the United States completely confirmed the propriety of the course pursued in soliciting that conference; and, though communicated informally, is entitled to great consideration, as affording evidence of views that have prevailed to our injury among the highest authorities. There are some allusions in my statement, which, on a cursory view, might be regarded as digressions; but they were introduced with the special object of replying to certain misrepresentations in the Report of the Secretary of Foreign Affairs, and of showing particularly that the Executive Decree requiring all con-

461508

signments of foreign goods to be made to citizens of
Colombia was not justified by the principle of reciprocity
adopted in the United States.

You will have observed an obvious negligence on the
part of the Executive in having failed when, from a regard to their own professions, to press the repeal of the
five per cent.; and the very reasons assigned by Congress
contradict, by inference, the opinion so confidently urged
in the accompanying letter of the Secretary of Foreign
Affairs of the Government entertaining the most friendly
feelings towards the United States. In this view of the
subject, it may be considered highly impolitic in this Government to regard the sense of gratitude toward the United
States for the recognition, instead of the immutable principles of justice, as a reason for the repeal of a law which
is indirectly acknowledged to have originated in the desire
of cultivating sentiments neither of peace nor friendship
toward the Government, whatever may have been their
feelings toward our *virtuous people* of the United States.

It gives me great pleasure to repeat the assurance of a
friendly feeling toward us pervading the mass of the people,
of the Congress, and a majority of the Executive; and if
they have ever entertained the prejudices, which still influence the conduct of the Secretary of Foreign Affairs, they
have forgotten them so far as not to suffer them to interfere
with their duty to both countries. Unfortunately, however,
for the United States, the leading men of this country have
formed their opinions upon certain assumed facts and principles not justified by the real attitude between the two countries. They have undertaken to suppose that there was a
perfect identity in the causes and consequences of the two
struggles, and have proceeded on the unwarrantable inference from this supposition that the United States, their elder
brother on the same continent, were bound to unite their
destinies with them; and thus not only involve their own
peace and safety, but encounter the general hostility of the
Powers of Europe. In the indulgence of their unreason-

able expectations, they appear to have forgotten that the United States, as a sovereign and independent power, were the sole judges of their duty and of the occasions in which it might be considered proper, if ever, to "abandon" their own, to stand "on foreign ground." The justice and prudence of their counsels in avoiding any measure which might involve them in the war, will necessarily impose on them the propriety of mature consideration before they form any other than commercial relations with this country. Indeed, the necessity of their deriving certain benefit against any possible designs by the European powers would alone justify any political connection with it.

With respect to the propriety of having conferred with the Vice-President, by the aid of one of the Judges of the Supreme Court, rather than that of the Secretary of Foreign Affairs, I might content myself with the remark that, as it was an unofficial interview, I was not only not required to maintain it through the Secretary of Foreign Affairs, but, having received information from the Judge of some of the circumstances rendering it necessary, there seemed to be a peculiar fitness in making the explanation through that channel. But I had, notwithstanding, abundant evidence of the indelicacy and inexpediency of committing it to the agency of the Secretary of Foreign Affairs,—the depreciating allusions in his letter of the 10th of May; the want of cordiality in his personal intercourse; his notorious unfriendliness towards the United States; the circumstances in my statement implicating his sincerity; a measure of the most extraordinary nature adopted by him while in the United States; his general character and the breach of confidence in causing his letters to me to be translated by a foreigner, who is distinguished for the jealousy and malignity with which he regards the United States, and the rights and interests of their citizens, although I had, with a view to avoid this circumstance, previously requested them to be translated by a Colombian, as there were not citizens of the United States in this capital. All these

circumstances precluded the hope of obtaining justice and
conciliation through his agency, and imposed on me the
imperious duty of avoiding any measure which might afford
him the opportunity of further deceptions, or of widening
the breach.

I have the honor of enclosing herewith a copy of a note
of the 28th ultimo from Mr. C. J. Bunkle, together with his
correspondence with the Secretary of the Treasury, and a
copy of two letters of the 30th ultimo from the Secretary of
Foreign Affairs, with their enclosures, by which you will be
advised officially of the repeal of the discrimination in the
Tariff to our prejudice,— and of a decree, by the Executive,
of the 18th September, 1821, respecting the seizure of a
portion of the cargo of the brig "America." On the supposition that the parties may not have transmitted to the
Department a copy of the proceedings in this case, I
have the honor of enclosing a copy of the several decrees
adopted by the authorities of Colombia, and known to
the interested prior to their application to the Government of the United States; together with that lately communicated, and purporting to have been authorized on the
18th September last. I cannot pretend, in the short space
of a letter, to unfold all the circumstances connected with
this transaction, and therefore content myself with men-
tioning the principal features. The cargo of the Brig
"America" consisted of sundry military supplies, to be
delivered, under contract, with this Government, and a
large amount of merchandise, chiefly East India. In consequence of the heavy duties on the importation, amounting
from various causes to fifty per cent. upon an extravagant
valuation, though at Augostua the duties of importation
did not exceed, at the same time, fifteen or twenty per cent.,
the supercargo determined to enter the goods for re-
exportation to the United States; but he was not permitted
to carry this resolution into effect, and the goods were required to be landed without delay. The public store-houses
not being sufficiently spacious, they were disembarked under

a special and written permission, and in the usual mode in open day, and deposited in the house of a private individual near to the custom-house. During the landing of the goods, the written permission, according to custom, was delivered to the officer who has the direction of that proceeding; but upon the trial, which was instituted on the ground of an attempt clandestinely to introduce the twenty-two cases of goods, contrary to law, this necessary document could not be produced. It was the duty and in the power of those who condemned, or procured the condemnation, of the goods, to have furnished the paper, and the result authorizes the irresistible conclusion that it was purposely withheld or destroyed. The seizure was made by the Government, and a condemnation had by General Montilla, with the advice of the assessor or judge, D. Gual, at present Secretary of Foreign Affairs, and according to the laws supposed at that time to be in force, a considerable portion of the proceeds of said seizure was divided between those officers. The supercargo was prevented from prosecuting an appeal to the superior board of the Treasury in this capital, by his passport being refused, as consequence of certain process issued against him by the collector for defamation, in stating the goods had been illegally condemned. As soon, however, as the sentence below had been confirmed in this capital, though in the absence and without an opportunity of defence by the supercargo, the proceedings for defamation were dismissed and the passport granted. But upon his arrival at Mompox, where he had engaged all the boats, his further progress was again arrested, for six weeks, by the impressment, under the order of General Montilla, of those boats for the transportation of a detachment of troops to quell an imaginary revolt at Ocana. The supercargo, at length, however, arrived in this capital, though after the expiration of six months, within which a rehearing could usually be had. Fortunately he succeeded, in consequence of the interference of the Attorney-General appointed by the Government, in procuring a

6

rehearing and reversal of the decision at Santa Martha. It may be pertinent here to remark that General Montilla, entertaining doubts of the legality of the proposed condemnation, required the written opinion of D. Castillo, the present Secretary of the Treasury, to showing that the Assessor, D. Gual, would be responsible for any error of opinion in the case, so that he is considered eventually liable for the principal, and whatever damages this Government may be compelled to pay for the irregular seizure and detention. The enclosed copy of the letter from Mr. C. J. Bunkle to his employers will show the measures he adopted to procure indemnification ; and that, after reference to all the Departments of the Government, as may be seen in the decrees, he finally requested the Executive to inform him, to what authority to make effectual application.

I have the most satisfactory assurances that the Department of the Treasury, if not of the members of the Government, were advised that Mr. Bunkle had left an agent in this capital with authority to receive the amount of the claim ;   and, on the 20th of March last, D. Gual was informed that I had received instructions from my Government to submit a claim in this case.   A copy of all the proceedings was accordingly enclosed with my despatch of 5th April.   The case, however, was not noticed by this Government, until his letter of the 4th June, in which, so far from intimating the existence of a subsequent decree on the 18th September by the Executive who had previously disavowed any authority to interfere in the sentence, the Secretary offered certain transferable debentures in payment as soon as the amount of the claim should be precisely ascertained.   He was informed, in my letter of the 16th June, of the exact amount to which the claim would be reduced ; and, although Mr. Bunkle has been in this capital since the 11th of May, this Government, with a knowledge of these circumstances, ventures on the indelicate and unwarrantable proceeding of endeavoring " to transfer the negotiations," by a communication on the 23d of June, through the Secretary of the Treasury, of a silent decree, to an individual who had irrevocably ceded all agency in the business — after his refusal, very properly, to enter into any discussion upon the subject. Received on the 1st July the letter and accompanying documents from the Secretary of Foreign Affairs.

It is not necessary, in this place, to animadvert on the nefarious complexion of the whole transaction, so derogatory to the good faith and integrity of the Government, or on the suspicious circumstances attending the development of the extraordinary decree of the 18th September, in the maintenance of which the Secretary of Foreign Affairs is individually so deeply interested. The merits of the controversy are forgotten in the unjustifiable act of attempting to withdraw the negotiations from the hands in which it had been legitimately vested by the Government of the United States and the parties concerned. At a more convenient time, I shall do myself the honor of developing all the circumstances connected with this case, and suggest, for the present, that the facts already noticed and the gross intimation conveyed in the concluding paragraph in the Secretary's letter of the 30th of June, have imposed on me the painful necessity of considering all further official intercourse, on my part, with this Government as at an end; and that, whilst the present Secretary continues to be the organ of this Government to foreign nations, no intercourse will be renewed, until the arrival of Mr. Anderson, or of further powers to myself. Indeed, the anxious solicitude I feel to avoid any act which might embarrass the attitude of Mr. Anderson, or the future views of the United States in relation to this country, alone prevents me demanding my passports immediately. It is proper, also, to apprise you that it is possible I may yet adopt this course, and that I may hesitate, even on the receipt of additional instructions, to renew the intercourse through D. Gual.

I have the honor to be

Your obedient servant,

C. S. Todd.

Hon. J. Q. Adams.

At the close of the mission to Colombia, in 1824, Colonel Todd returned to the United States, and established himself upon a tract of land in Shelby County, originally located by Governor Shelby. It is no exaggeration to say that Colonel Todd made his farm the most valuable in the State. He introduced Blue grass into the woods, and introduced the first blooded cattle. When he took charge of this tract of land, it could not have been sold for more than five dollars per acre; but his improved system of cultivation soon made it worth from fifty to sixty dollars per acre.

Indeed, his knowledge of farming became so widely known that he was chosen President of the State Agricultural Society. The pages of many of our most prominent agricultural journals and magazines are enriched with able and interesting articles from his pen. In January, 1839, he delivered an address before the State Agricultural Society, which was very generally read and admired. Some years ago it was republished in a Louisville paper, and attracted almost as much attention as if it had been written at a more recent period. I have been unable to get a copy of it, or I should certainly have included it in this memoir.

CHAPTER VI.

The Harrison Campaign — Colonel Todd one of its Master - Spirits — He Removes to Cincinnati, and takes Charge of the *Cincinnati Republican* — He Speaks as well as Writes — He, in Conjunction with Benjamin Drake, Prepares a Life of General Harrison — Extracts from this Work — Incidents of the Campaign.

ONE of the most interesting events in the life of Colonel Todd is the part that he enacted in the election of General Harrison to the Presidency. As soon as Harrison was nominated, Colonel Todd removed to Cincinnati, Ohio, and took charge of the *Cincinnati Republican*, then one of the most influential Whig papers in the State. Besides attending to his arduous editorial duties, he addressed the people in nearly all the large cities and towns in the West. He was also employed, in conjunction with Benjamin Drake, an able and effective writer, by the Whig Central Committees of Ohio and Kentucky, to prepare a Life of General Harrison. The work was soon completed. It consisted of a small volume of one hundred and seventy pages. It was published by G. P. James, of Cincinnati. Many thousand copies were sold. It was used as a campaign document, and as a sort of text-book by the leading politicians and journalists of the country. It is divided into thirteen chapters, written alternately by Colonel Todd and Mr. Drake. So nearly did the styles of these two writers resemble one another, that it was a subject of curious inquiry which parts of the book were written by Colonel Todd and which by Mr. Drake.

At my solicitation, Colonel Todd pointed out the chapters from his pen.

The Introduction to the book is the joint work of both. The first chapter, (an extract of which I subjoin, giving an account of the education and early life of General Harrison, his entrance into the army, and of the battle of Maumee, etc.,) Colonel Todd wrote. It will enable the reader to form a very correct idea of the character of the work.

" WM. HENRY HARRISON was educated at Hampden Sydney College, and then repaired to Philadelphia to pursue the study of medicine under the instruction of the distinguished Dr. Benjamin Rush, and under the guardianship of Robert Morris, the great financier of the Revolution, both of whom were signers of the Declaration of Independence. The youth, who had laid the foundations at college for a taste in the literature and history of the ancient classics, was thus afforded an opportunity of drinking deep at these fountains of the genius and spirit of the Revolution. He had derived from his patriotic father the lessons of republican liberty, and in the school of *Rush*, of *Morris*, and of *Washington*, he imbibed a love of country, which led him to encounter difficulty and danger in her defence. About this period the disasters of the Northwestern army, under the accomplished Harmar, excited a deep sympathy in the public mind, and the youthful Harrison, partaking largely of the generous impulses of the day, resolved to abandon the studies in which he was engaged, and to participate in the perils as well as the sacrifices which were incident to this great border warfare. His guardian

and his friends opposed his wish to enter upon this
hazardous duty; but he applied in person to General
Knox, Secretary of War, and to the IMMORTAL WASH-
INGTON, who granted him a commission of ensign in
the first regiment of the United States Artillery; and
in November, 1791, when but nineteen years of age,
he marched on foot to Pittsburg, and, by descending
the Ohio, joined his regiment, then stationed at Fort
Washington.   Shortly before the disastrous defeat
of the veteran St.·Clair, ensign Harrison formed the
resolution to devote his energies to the military service of his country, at a period when his judgment
and feelings must have been guided by a high sense
of patriotism, and a disinterested love of fame. The
theatre of the war was in the remote wilderness, and
the character of the enemy such that laurels were to
be won only by great suffering and exposure in situations destitute of the comforts or even the necessa-
ries of civilized life.   A great national disaster had
occurred in 1790, under the gallant Harmar, who was
seconded by the heroic conduct of Colonel Hardin,
himself a sacrifice to the treachery of the Indian character.   Congress authorized, at its next session, the
raising of two thousand men, under the denomination
of levies; and General St. Clair, governor of the
Northwestern territories, was appointed commander-
in-chief. On the 4th of November, 1791, he was met
and likewise defeated, with great loss, by a formidable body of Indians, on the waters of the Big Miami
River. This defeat of St. Clair, though Congress
subsequently acquitted him of all blame, produced a
deep impression on the public mind, and, connected
with the previous disasters of the war, rendered the

service unpopular, drained the public treasury, and brought the country into a crisis which developed the energies of Washington's great intellect. The war had assumed a national importance, inducing the President to select for the chief of the army a soldier of prudence, of experience, and of energy. The choice was balanced for a time between Clarke and Wayne, both distinguished leaders in the war of the Revolution, though on a different theatre: the former acting under the immediate eye of the father of his country, earning for himself the reputation of intrepidity, with fertility of expedient; the latter having won the distinctive title of the *Hannibal of the West*. The command was eventually assigned to Wayne, who acquired a new wreath of glory for himself, and added to the proofs of the sagacity of Washington. Ensign Harrison joined his regiment at Fort Washington, just in time to witness the return of the fragments of that gallant band, which, marching out in the proud anticipation of victory, was destined to a sad reverse under the veteran St. Clair. Under these discouraging circumstances, and with the near approach of winter, Ensign Harrison commenced his public service in the command of an escort having charge of a train of pack-horses destined for Fort Hamilton. It was a duty involving peril and fatigue by night and by day, and requiring the exercise of sagacity and self-denial. His performance of the arduous task elicited the commendations of General St. Clair, and exhibited an interesting instance of a character in which the ardor of youth was combined with the maturity of age. In 1792 he was promoted to the rank of lieutenant, and in 1793 joined the legion

under General Wayne, and was not long afterwards
selected by him as one of his aids-de-camp, — illus-
trating, in an eminent degree, the confidence of that
tried soldier, since Lieutenant Harrison was only
twenty-one years of age. He continued to act as aid
to General Wayne during the whole of the ensuing
campaign, receiving, as he merited, repeated instances
of high encomium from his commander. The first
occurred upon the occasion of a detachment having
been sent on the 23d of December, 1793, to take
possession of the field of battle of the 4th 'of November, 1791, and to fortify the position. To the new
post was given the name of Fort Recovery. The
following general order was issued on the return of
the troops from that interesting duty: 'The Commander-in-Chief returns his most grateful thanks to
Major Henry Burbeck, and to every officer, non-
commissioned officer, and private, belonging to the
detachment under his command, for their soldierly and
exemplary good conduct during their late arduous
tour of duty, and the cheerfulness with which they
surmounted every difficulty, at this inclement season,
in repossessing General St. Clair's field of battle, and
erecting thereon *Fort Recovery*, a work impregnable
by savage force; as also for piously and carefully
collecting and interring the bones, and paying the
last respect and military honors to the remains of
the heroes who fell on the 4th of November, 1791, by
three times three discharges from the *same artillery*
that was lost on that fatal day, but now recovered by
this detachment of the legion. The Commander-in-
Chief also requests Major Mills, Captains De Butts
and Butler, *Lieutenant Harrison*, and Dr. Scott, to

7

accept his best thanks for their voluntary aid and
services on this occasion.'

"The other instance of commendation of the gallantry of Lieut. Harrison is to be found in the report
made by General Wayne to the War Department,
in relation to the celebrated battle of the Maumee,
which we shall presently introduce to the notice of
the reader. The youth, the early habits of study,
and the delicate frame of Mr. Harrison, not less than
the perils and privations incident to the border warfare, would have intimidated a spirit less heroic than
his, in entering upon the arduous service in the
Northwest. As illustrative of the aspect of affairs,
and of his first appearance in the army, an old soldier of St. Clair, who was present, has remarked : 'I
would as soon have thought of putting my wife in
the service as this boy; but I have been out with
him, and I find those smooth cheeks are on a wise
head, and that slight frame is almost as tough as my
own weather-beaten carcass.' General Charles Scott,
a veteran of the Revolution, who enjoyed the special
confidence of Washington, arrived in July from Kentucky with his command of mounted volunteers; and,
on the 8th of August, General Wayne took up a
position at Grand Glaize, seventy miles in advance
of Greenville. A strong work was erected at the
junction of the Auglaize and Maumee rivers, and
General Wayne again opened a communication with
the Indians before striking the final blow. 'I have
thought proper,' he said, 'to offer the enemy a last
overture of peace; and, as they have everything that is
dear and interesting at stake, I have reason to expect
they will listen to the proposition mentioned in the

enclosed copy of an address dispatched yesterday by
a special flag, under circumstances that will insure
his safe return, and which may eventually spare the
effusion of much human blood. But, should war be
their choice, that blood be upon their own heads.
America shall no longer be insulted with impunity.
To an all-powerful and just God, I therefore com-
mit myself and gallant army.' The enemy rejected
the offer of peace; and the celebrated Little Turtle,
who advised its adoption in a council on the night
before the battle, spoke as follows: ' We have beaten
the enemy twice under separate commanders. We
cannot expect the same good fortune to attend us
always. The Americans are now led by a chief who
never sleeps; the night and the day are alike to him.
And during all the time he has been marching upon
our villages, notwithstanding the watchfulness of our
young men, we have never been able to surprise him.
Think well of it. There is something whispers me,
it would be prudent to listen to his offers of peace.'
We refer the reader to the official report of General
Wayne, of the 27th of August, 1794, for a perspicuous
account of the celebrated battle of *Maumee*, and deem
it sufficient for our present purpose to give an extract
relating to the conduct of his aid-de-camp, Lieutenant
Harrison : ' The bravery and conduct of every officer
belonging to the army, from the generals down to
the ensigns, merit my highest approbation. There
were, however, some whose rank and situation placed
their conduct in a very conspicuous point of view,
and which I observed with pleasure and with the
most lively gratitude: among whom I beg leave to
mention Brigadier - General Wilkinson and Colonel

Hamtramck, the commandants of the right and left wings of the legion, whose brave example inspired the troops; and to these I must add the names of my faithful and gallant aids-de-camp, Captains De Butts and T. Lewis, and *Lieutenant Harrison, who,* with the Adjutant-general, Major Mills, *rendered the most essential service by communicating my orders in every direction, and by their conduct and bravery exciting the troops to press for victory.'* The praise of which lieutenant, now General Harrison, was the subject in the despatch from the illustrious Wayne, was of a character to soothe him for the trials and the perils he had encountered, and to stimulate him to increased diligence in the discharge of the high and responsible duties confided to him when placed afterwards in the command of Fort Washington. This commendation received additional weight from the remarks made in the presence of a venerable gentleman, now living, by General Wilkinson and Colonel Shaumburg, who said that 'Harrison was in the foremost front of the hottest battle; his person was exposed from the commencement to the close of the action. Wherever duty called, he hastened, regardless of danger; and by his efforts and example contributed as much to secure the fortune of the day as any other officer subordinate to the Commander-in-Chief.' The victory *at Maumee* was achieved by the discipline of Wayne's army, and the introduction by that sagacious leader of a new feature in military tactics as applied to Indian warfare, which was the result of a plan digested by Washington, Knox, and Wayne. The Northwestern savage chooses his own time and his own position, and he retreats from it at his own pleasure. To be overcome, he must be outflanked or kept on the wing, as he was by Wayne, by a constant charge of the bayonet. To provide against the contingency of the enemy assailing his flanks, Wayne had adopted the plan of forming his troops at open order, so as to extend his flanks and move with celerity in the woods. These principles were acted upon in the subsequent war conducted by General Harrison, and may be now regarded as the approved mode of fighting the Northwestern Indians. A permanent peace with the Indians was the fruit of this great victory. The negotiations commenced in January and terminated in August, 1795. Soon after the close of this campaign, Captain Harrison was intrusted by Wayne with the command of Fort Washington, where he was directed to advise the general of all movements connected with the invasion of Louisiana, then projected, and to prevent the forwarding of any military stores by the French agents. As a further evidence of the confidence of Wayne, he specially entrusted Captain Harrison with his commands, and intentions as to the supply of the troops intended to occupy the posts theretofore held by the British on the Northern frontier. While in the command of Fort Washington (now Cincinnati), Captain Harrison married the daughter of John Cleves Symmes, the founder of the Miami settlements. An anecdote is given in relation to the marriage, illustrative of the independent character of Captain Harrison. On the proposal to Mr. Symmes for his consent, Harrison was asked what were his resources for maintaining a wife? Placing his hand upon his sword, he replied, 'This, sir, is my support!' The

chivalry and undaunted confidence of the young sol-
dier at once obtained the approbation of Mr. Symmes.
Captain Harrison continued in the command of Fort
Washington until 1797, when, upon the death of
General Wayne, he resigned his commission in the
army."

The succeeding chapters give a very thorough
account of his being appointed Secretary of the
Northwestern Territory, and afterward a delegate to
Congress ; and of his great efforts in securing the
passage of a law putting an end to the system of
selling the public lands in large tracts to speculators,
contrary to the interest of the poor man. The law
met with a great deal of opposition, both in the
Senate and in the House of Representatives. Harrison had such a perfect knowledge of the evils of
the old law, and the justice of the proposed one, that
he finally succeeded in securing its passage. We
are informed in this *Life of Harrison*, that, in the
subsequent legislation of Congress regulating the
sales of the public lands, all the features of Harrison's original report and bill upon the subject were
incorporated. The fourth chapter of this little work
contains an account of an interview between Harrison and Tecumseh, the celebrated Indian chief, and
also a very interesting account of the battle of Tippecanoe. This chapter is also from the pen of Colonel
Todd. It is so good that we cannot resist repro-
ducing it here :

"Between the years 1806 and 1811, Governor
Harrison's duties, as superintendent of Indian affairs,

were delicate and responsible. During this period, the British agents were powerfully aided in their efforts to excite the Indians to hostility against the United States by two remarkable individuals, Tecumseh and his brother Olliwachica, better known as the Prophet. The genius of the one and the prophetical character of the other drew around them a band of desperate followers, who finally established themselves at Tippecanoe. The treaty made at Fort Wayne, in 1809, by Governor Harrison, gave offence to Tecumseh, it being in violation of the great principle of his confederacy, that the Indian lands were the common property of all the tribes, and could not be sold without the consent of all. In August, 1810, he invited Tecumseh to visit Vincennes, to have the difficulties adjusted. The chief, attended by four hundred warriors, armed with war-clubs and tomahawks, presented themselves at the appointed time. It was at this council that Tecumseh declared the Governor's statements false, and sprung to his arms; his example being followed by forty of his warriors, who were present at the conference. The firmness of the Governor, and the final termination of this extraordinary interview, must be familiar to the reader. It was at the close of this council, when, upon Governor Harrison's telling him that he would refer the question between them to the President, that Tecumsch replied, 'Well, as the great chief is to determine the matter, I hope the Great Spirit will put sense enough into his head to induce him to direct you to give up this land. It is true, he is so far off, he will not be injured by the war; he may sit still in his town, and drink his wine, while you and I will

have to fight it out.' The Governor, in conclusion,
told Tecumseh that he had one proposal to make,
and that was, in the event of a war, to put a stop to
that cruel and disgraceful mode of warfare which the
Indians were accustomed to wage against women and
children, and upon their prisoners. To this proposition, resulting from Governor Harrison's benevolent
forecast, he cheerfully assented, and it is due to the
memory of Tecumseh to add that he faithfully kept
his promise. Tecumseh left Vincennes, boldly avowing his determination to persevere in his efforts to
combine the tribes, on the principle already alluded
to; and, in the next year, he visited the Southern
Indians for this purpose, leaving the Prophet in
charge of the party at Tippecanoe, but with instructions to avoid an open rupture with the United States
during his absence. In the summer of 1811, the
danger to the frontier became so imminent that the
President placed some troops under the command
of Governor Harrison, to be used offensively, however, in such a contingency only as in his judgment
he might deem indispensably necessary. Governor
Harrison consulted with Governors Howard and
Edwards, of Missouri and Illinois, who advised the
breaking up of the Prophet's town, or, at all events,
the prevention of the further assemblage of Indians
at that point. The Governor's force consisted of
regulars and militia, a small part of the latter being
from Kentucky, with whom came Daviess, Croghan,
O'Fallon, Shipp, Meade, Edwards, and Saunders,—
gallant young volunteers, who not only distinguished
themselves in the action which ensued, but performed
a brilliant part in the subsequent war with Great

Britain. The Governor was also joined by Owen and Wells, both celebrated in the early history of Kentucky. Passing over the intermediate details, the Governor, on the evening of the 6th of November, with a force of nine hundred men, was within a mile and a half of the Prophet's town, where he halted the army, to make a final effort to prevent the necessity of an attack. This effort proved unavailing. The army then marched toward the village. This led to a conference with the Indians, who announced their pacific intentions, and agreed that the terms of peace should be settled on the following day. A halt was ordered, and Majors Waller Taylor and Marston Clark, and Colonel William Piatt, were directed to examine and select a suitable spot for an encampment. The two former reported that they had found a place, combining all that could be desired, on the bank of a small stream, nearly surrounded by an open prairie, on the north of the town. On this spot, late in the evening of the 6th, the army was encamped. The details of the severe and brilliant action which took place on the following morning are familiar to the reading public. We have not space to give them. The Indians made a fierce and gallant attack, but were as gallantly met, and finally compelled to retreat. The officers and soldiers acted with great bravery, and were specially noticed in the official letter of the Commander-in-Chief. The number of men killed, including those who died of their wounds, was upwards of fifty; the wounded were more than double that number. The loss of the Indians, in killed, was about the same with that of the whites. They left thirty-eight dead on the field of battle. Some were

8

buried in the town, and others, it is supposed, died of
their wounds subsequently. The force of Governor
Harrison, on the day of action, amounted to about
nine hundred. The traders estimated the Indian force
at from eight hundred to one thousand men. Captain
Wells, the Indian agent, assured a gentleman from
Ohio, now living, that several of the Indians engaged
in the battle, who visited Fort Wayne after the action, stated their number to have been near twelve
hundred, and that the proportion of wounded was
unusually great. It is an act of justice to the Commander-in-Chief to add, that a ball passed through
his cravat, bruising his neck, and another struck his
saddle, and then hit his thigh. The horse on which
he rode was severely wounded in the head. No
battle ever fought in the United States has been more
extensively examined or severely criticised than the
battle of Tippecanoe. Soon after its occurrence, the
enemies of Governor Harrison severely censured his
conduct, and charged upon him that he permitted the
Indians to select his camping-ground, and was taken
by surprise on the morning of the attack. These
charges, although generally discredited, and made
by irresponsible persons, called out the testimony of
the officers and men engaged in the action, and thus
placed all the facts before the public. In regard to
the first of these charges, General Waller Taylor, of
Indiana, under date of 15th of July, 1823, says : 'The
Indians did not dictate to the Governor the position
to encamp the army the night before the battle of
Tippecanoe. After the army reached the Indian town,
in the afternoon, perhaps about sunset, the Governor
ordered Major Clark and myself to proceed to the

left, and endeavor to find a suitable place for encampment; we did so, and discovered the place upon
which the battle was fought the next morning; upon
our return to the army, we reported to the Governor
our opinion about the place, which we stated to be
favorable for an encampment.' This statement is
corroborated by Colonel Wm. Piatt, late of Cincinnati, who was also in the action. Major Charles
Larrabee, a brave officer, who was also present, says,
under date of 13th October, 1823: 'Three officers,
well able to judge, went out in search of a place, and
they reported the one taken up. The situation was
such that, if the army had been called upon to make
choice of a place to fight the Indians, I venture to
say, nine-tenths would have made that their selection.' In the year following, General Hopkins, of
Kentucky, a Revolutionary officer, while on an expedition against the Peoria towns in Indiana, visited
the battle-ground of Tippecanoe, and expressed the
opinion that the spot on which General Harrison
encamped was the *best* in the neighborhood of the
Prophet's town. In this opinion the officers of this
expedition concurred; and such, we are authorized
to say, has been the fact with many military men
who have since visited the scene of action. In reply
to the second charge, Joel Cook, Josiah Snelling,
R. C. Barton, O. G. Burton, Nathaniel F. Adams,
Charles Fuller, A. Hawkins, George Gooding, H.
Burchstead, Josiah D. Foster, and Hosea Bloodgood,
all of them officers of the Fourth Regiment, United
States Infantry, and in the battle of Tippecanoe, say,
under their own proper hands: 'We deem it our duty
to state, as incontestable facts, that the Commander-

in-Chief throughout the campaign, and in the hour of
battle, proved himself the soldier and the general; that
on the night of the action, by his order, we slept on our
arms, and rose on our posts; that, notwithstanding the
darkness of the night, and the most consummate savage cunning of the enemy in eluding our sentries, and
rapidity in rushing through the guards, we were not
found unprepared; that few of the men were able to
enter our camp, and those few doomed never to return;
that, in pursuance of his orders, which were adapted
to every emergency, the enemy were defeated with a
slaughter almost unparalleled among savages. Indeed,
one sentiment of confidence, respect, and affection
toward the Commander-in-Chief, pervaded the whole
line of the army, any attempt to destroy which we
shall consider as an insult to our understandings, and
an injury to our feelings.' Major Larrabee, under
date of Fort Knox, January 8th, 1812, says: 'At the
commencement of the action, my company were at
rest in their tents, with their clothes and accoutre-
ments on, their guns lying by their sides, loaded, and
bayonets fixed, and were by my order paraded in line
'of battle, ready to meet the enemy within forty sec-
onds from the commencement of the action, all of
which was performed one or two minutes before a
man of the company was wounded.' The officers
and non-commissioned officers and privates of the
militia corps (Hargrave's excepted) of Knox County,
in Indiana, who served in this campaign, held a meeting in Vincennes, 7th December, 1811, and passed
the following resolutions, unanimously: 'That it is a
notorious fact, known to the whole army, that all the
changes of position made by the troops during the

action of the 7th ultimo, and by which the victory was secured, were made by the direction of the Commander-in-Chief, and generally executed under his immediate superintendence.' 'That it was owing to the skill and VALOR of the Commander-in-Chief, that the victory of Tippecanoe was obtained.' 'That we have the most perfect confidence in the Commander-in-Chief, and shall always feel a cheerfulness in serving under him, whenever the exigency of the country may require it.' General Thomas Scott, of Indiana, under date of Vincennes, July 25, 1823, says: 'I have thought, and still think, that few generals would have faced danger at so many points as General Harrison did in the action of Tippecanoe. Wherever the action was warmest, was General Harrison to be found, and heard encouraging and cheering the officers and soldiers.' Mr. Adam Walker, of Keene, New Hampshire, a printer by profession, who was in the action, says, in his published journal: 'General Harrison received a shot through the rim of his hat. In the heat of the action his voice was frequently heard and easily distinguished, giving his orders in the same calm, cool, and collected manner, with which we had been used to receive them on drill or parade. The confidence of the troops in the General was unlimited.' General John O'Fallon, now residing in St.Louis, a nephew of General George Rogers Clark, and a gallant officer of the late war, having distinguished himself at the siege of Fort Meigs and the battle of the Thames, in a late speech, at a public meeting in that city, in speaking of General Harrison, says: 'At the age of nineteen, I first became acquainted with the distinguished patriot, in whose behalf we have

assembled, and having been by his side through
nearly the whole of the late war, I can bear testimony
to his cool, undaunted, and collected courage, as well
as to his skill, as an able, efficient, and active officer.
After the battle of Tippecanoe, which has thrown so
much glory over our country's arms, *it was universally
admitted, that General Harrison was the only officer
that could have saved the army from defeat and mas-
sacre.'* In dismissing this part of our subject, it is proper
to say that, at the commencement. of the attack, the
Commander-in-Chief had risen, and was seated by the
fire in conversation with Wells, Taylor, Owen, and
Hurst, the three latter his aids-de-camp, and the
former commanding the mounted riflemen. These
individuals had been awakened by their commander,
before four o'clock, and preparations were making at
the moment of the attack for the troops generally to
turn out. Additional testimony of a high and unim-
peachable character might, if necessary, be adduced
to repel the charge of Governor Harrison's having
been taken by surprise. Another charge inculcated
against the Commander-in-Chief, is, that he put the
gallant Daviess on his white horse, in consequence
of which that officer lost his life. In reply to this
unfounded allegation, it is only necessary to say, that
Major Daviess was killed while bravely charging on
foot, and that he was not on General Harrison's horse,
nor any other horse, during the engagement. This
charge has been varied, so as to make Owen instead
of Daviess the individual who was killed on General
Harrison's white horse. This is equally untrue. Owen
was killed upon his own white horse, and was not at
any time during the action on either of General Har-

rison's horses. The facts, in this case, have been stated, distinctly, by the Commander-in-Chief, in a letter to Dr. Scott, of Frankfort, Ky.: 'I had in the campaign, for my own riding, a gray mare and a sorrel horse. They were both fine riding-nags, but the mare was uncommonly spirited and active. I generally rode them, alternately, day and day about. On the day we got to the town, I was on the mare, and as it was our invariable rule to have the horses saddled and bridled through the night, the saddle was kept upon her; and, like other horses belonging to my family, she was tied to a picket driven into the ground, in the rear of my marquee, and between that and the baggage-wagon. In the night the mare pulled up the picket and got loose. The dragoon sentinel awakening my servant George, the latter caught the mare, and tied her to the wagon-wheel on the back side. When the alarm took place, I called for the mare. George, being aroused from his sleep, and confoundedly frightened, forgot that he had removed her to the other side of the wagon, and was unable to find her. In the mean time, Major Taylor's servant had brought up his horse. The major observed that I had better mount him, and that he would get another, and follow me. I did so. Poor Owen accompanied me, mounted upon a remarkably white horse. Before we got to the angle which was first attacked, Owen was killed. I, at that time, supposed that it was a ball which had passed over the heads of the infantry that had killed him ; but I am persuaded that he was killed by one of the two Indians who got within the lines, and that it was extremely probable that they mistook him for me. Taylor joined me in a few minutes after,

mounted on my gray mare. I immediately directed
him to go and get another. He returned to my
quarters, and preferring my sorrel horse to another
of his own that was there, mounted him, and we thus
continued on each other's horses till near the close of
the action. Being then with both my aids-de-camp,
Taylor and Hurst, in the rear of the right flank line,
the fire of several Indians near to the line was directed
at us. One of their balls killed the horse that Taylor
was riding, and another passed through the sleeve of
his coat; a third wounded the horse I was riding in
the head, and a fourth was very near terminating my
earthly career.' In December, 1811, the Legislative
Council and House of Representatives of the Indiana
Territory presented an address to Governor Harrison
in reference to the battle of Tippecanoe, in which they
bear testimony to his 'superior capacity,' 'integrity,'
and 'other qualities which adorn the mind in a super-
lative degree.' In December, 1811, the Hon. John
J. Crittenden moved the following Resolution in the
Legislature of Kentucky, which, after being fully discussed, was carried with only two or three dissenting
votes: '*Resolved*, That, in the late campaign against
the Indians on the Wabash, Governor Wm. Henry
Harrison has, in the opinion of this Legislature, be-
haved like a hero, a patriot, and a general; and that, for
his cool, deliberate, skilful, and gallant conduct in the
late battle of Tippecanoe, he well deserves the warmest thanks of the nation.' This Resolution was approved by Governor Scott. President Madison, on
the 18th of December, 1811, in a message to Congress,
says, in regard to this battle: 'While it is deeply
lamented that so many valuable lives have been lost

in the action which took place on the 7th ultimo,
Congress will see with satisfaction the dauntless spirit
and fortitude displayed by every description of the
troops engaged, as well as the collected firmness which
distinguished their commander on an occasion requiring the utmost exertion of valor and discipline.'
M'Affee, in his History of the Late War, says: 'After
much altercation, by which the battle of Tippecanoe
was fought over again, and fully investigated, in all
the public circles of the Western country, the public
opinion preponderated greatly in favor of the Governor. All the material accusations of his enemies
were disproved; and, after all the testimony had
been heard, the common opinion seemed to be, that
the army had been conducted with prudence, and that
the battle had been fought as well as it could have
been by any general, considering the time and manner of the attack.' Dawson, in his Life of Harrison,
says: 'The battle of Tippecanoe had a different
character from any one that had ever before been
fought with the Indians. A victory had never been
obtained over them where the force on both sides was
nearly equal; and in no battle that had ever before
been fought with them, were there so many killed in
proportion to the number engaged.' The same writer
adds: 'That mutual confidence, which ought always
to subsist between the commander of an army and
the troops commanded, perhaps never had been in a
higher degree manifested than at the battle of Tippecanoe. Wherever his presence was required during
the action, there was the Governor to be found. The
plan he had laid down previous to the battle was so
well understood by his men, that, notwithstanding the

9

enemy was not really expected that night, within less than two minutes after the first fire was heard every man was at his post.' Judge Hall, himself an officer in the late war with Great Britain, in speaking of the battle of Tippecanoe, says : ' As far as any commander is entitled to credit, independent of his army, he (General Harrison) merits and has received it.   He shared every danger and fatigue to which his army was exposed.   In the battle he was in more peril than any other individual; for he was personally known to every Indian, and exposed himself fearlessly on horse-back, at all points of the attack, during the whole en-gagement.   Every important movement was made by his express order.'   Finally, we take leave of this subject, in the language of the same eloquent writer : ' The field of Tippecanoe has become classic ground ; the American traveller pauses there to contemplate a scene which has become hallowed by victory ; the people of Indiana contemplate with pride the battle-ground on which their militia won imperishable honor, and their infant State became enrolled in the ranks of patriotism.' "

This work formed the basis of all the succeeding Lives of Harrison.   Colonel Todd included in it the peroration of the General's famous speech on Kosci-usko, and an extract from his speech on Jackson's conduct in the Seminole War.   This last contains the passage so often quoted about the age of deification being past, and about Jackson living in the songs of the virgins, and the Constitution of the country remaining immortal.   This speech is remarkable for its bold criticism on Jackson's policy, and its defence of such of the acts of that distinguished citizen as Harrison thought right. It is gratifying to me to know that Harrison did not think favorably of the institution of slavery, — that great blot upon the fair fame of our country. He did not grapple with this question, as did the statesmen of a later period; but he acknowledged the evil, and said that we must wait "the slow but certain progress of those good principles which are everywhere gaining ground, and which assuredly will ultimately prevail."

Colonel Todd also gives us Harrison's opinion on duelling, another wretched and barbarous practice, not yet wholly without its advocates in many parts of our country. General Harrison said that "the wealth and honor of the world would not tempt him to level a pistol at the breast of a man whom he had injured." He also said that, while he was in command of the Northwestern army, he declared his determination to punish, by all means that the military laws placed in his hands, any injury, or even insult, which should be offered by the superior to the inferior officer, and that during his entire command he had the satisfaction of knowing that not a single duel had been fought in his army, or even a challenge given. He said, in 1838, in a letter to a gentleman from New Jersey, who had addressed him on the subject: "In relation to my present sentiments, a sense of higher obligations than human laws or human opinions can impose, has determined me, never, on any occasion, to accept a challenge or seek redress for a personal injury by a resort to the laws which compose the code of honor."

These passages from the Life of Harrison, by

Colonel Todd and Mr. Drake, are very interesting, and embrace nearly all the important events in the life of that great and good man up to the time of his nomination for the Presidency in 1840. The book well deserved the large circulation it had, and should, I think, be published again.

Colonel Todd wrote the concluding chapter, in which Harrison's claims to the office of President of the United States are ably set forth:

"Our narrative," says the writer, in conclusion, "of the civil and military services of Harrison is now closed. Brief and imperfect as it may appear, it is sufficient to establish his claim to a high rank as a civilian and a general. He has been thoroughly tried in the council and in the field, and in every situation has proved himself equal to the circumstances by which he has been surrounded. No citizen of the United States, it is believed, has ever filled so many civil and military offices as the subject of this memoir; and certainly no one has ever been more uniformly successful in discharging the trusts confided to him. If it be true that to plan and carry on a successful campaign 'requires an almost intuitive sagacity, great powers of combination, with prudence, caution, promptness, and energy, combined with perfect self-reliance and self-control,' it may be assumed that General Harrison, who is admitted to possess these attributes, is an accomplished civil ruler; inasmuch as these are precisely the qualities which fit an individual for acting efficiently upon men and things as they exist around them. But there are other and more practical evidences of his capacity as a statesman. More than twenty years of his life have been spent in various important *civil* offices, many of them requiring inflexible integrity, firmness, intelligence, and wisdom. To prove that he possesses these virtues in a high degree, it is only necessary to recur to his acts as Governor of Indiana, as Indian Commissioner, and as a member of the national legislature. The messages, letters, and speeches, called forth by these different situations, are not only fine specimens of composition, but exhibit great accuracy of information, consistency of political principle, and maturity of judgment. Rising above all sectarian or party influence, his views were at once national and deeply imbued with the love of liberty; his voice and influence have ever been exerted in sustaining the cause of freedom in this as well as other kindred lands. In his military capacity, General Harrison is not less distinguished. As Commander-in-Chief of the North-western army, he was entrusted with more extensive and responsible powers than have been confided to any officer in our country, Washington alone excepted. The command assigned to him embraced an immense extent of territory, with a frontier of several hundred miles in length, stretching along the lakes (then in possession of the enemy), with harbors, inlets, and rivers, admirably suited to favor their attacks upon our scattered border settlements. To defend this extended line of frontier, the commander's forces were chiefly undisciplined militia — entirely wanting experience in the field — engaged for short terms of service, and held in obedience more by personal influence than the force of authority. But it was not to the *defence* alone of this district that General Harrison's duties were confined. He was directed by his Government to act *offensively* against the enemy, by retaking Detroit, and capturing the uppermost Canada, defended, as it was, by experienced British officers and soldiers, aided by a large body of Northwestern Indians. Detroit and Canada were separated from General Harrison's source of troops, munitions of war, and provisions, by a trackless and swampy wilderness, without roads, and presenting almost insuperable obstacles to the transportation of army supplies, while, at the same time, it was precisely the region of country best adapted to the peculiar mode of warfare practised by the bold and ferocious Indians. Notwithstanding these manifold difficulties, in about one year from the time when he was invested with the chief command of the Northwestern army, General Harrison drove the enemy from his extended military district, retook Detroit, defeated the combined army of Proctor and Tecumseh, on the Thames, conquered the uppermost Canada, and passed, as a victorious chieftain, down to the seat of war on the Niagara frontier. In many points, the military career of Harrison bears a strong analogy to that of Washington. The same extent of discretionary powers and responsibilities; the same difficulties in procuring supplies of troops and provisions ; and, in part, the same obstacles in the nature of the country to be traversed, marked the history of both. They never hazarded the grand result by a minor enterprise, however tempting ; they sought no laurels by the wanton sacrifice of their soldiers, but regulated all their movements with a single aim to the public good. Both exercised the extensive powers with which they were invested without any invasion of the laws or the rights of the citizen, and both retired to the peaceful pursuits of agriculture when the object which called them to the field had been effected; finally, to both may be justly awarded the valor of Marcellus, the caution of Fabius, and the disinterestedness of Cincinnatus. Inflexible integrity and a self-sacrificing patriotism may be considered the crowning virtues of General Harrison's character. These virtues have marked his career in the council and in the field, in youth and in age. When asked by what means he was enabled so successfully to gain the love and obedience of the militia, who followed his banner during the late war, he replied: 'By treating them with affection and kindness — by always recollecting that they were my fellow-citizens, whose feelings I was bound to respect, and by sharing with them, on every occasion, the hardships which they were obliged to undergo.' Throughout the whole of his military campaigns, he shared with his soldiers in all their fatigues, dangers, and privations. We were lately assured by a member of his military family in the campaign of 1813, that the table of the Commander-in-Chief was often not as well supplied with provisions as those of the common soldiers; and that he has frequently seen the General sitting by the fire roasting a piece of beef, and then eating it without salt or bread. On one occasion, after marching all day through a beech bottom covered with mud and water, without their baggage or any provisions, the General, by way of preventing his troops from being discouraged, sat down upon a log, wrapped in his cloak, — the rain falling fast, and the gloom of a night in the wilderness only broken by a

few glimmering camp-fires, — and then gaily calling
upon the officers to sing songs, he spread content
and cheerfulness throughout the whole detachment.
By examples such as these, he gained the confidence
and affection of the crowds of volunteer militia, who
were attracted to his standard not less by their patriotism as by the distinguished reputation of the Commander - in - Chief.   Since his retirement from the
army, he has been the chief representative of the
military class of our citizens in the region in which
he lives.   Those who served under him in the late
war make frequent pilgrimages to North Bend;
while the old soldiers, who fought under Harmar,
and St. Clair, and Wayne, not only throng his hospitable fireside, but look to General Harrison, above
all other men, to present their claims to Congress
for land or pensions on the score of past services
and sacrifices.   While Governor of Indiana and
Superintendent of Indian Affairs during a period of
twelve years, he disbursed at his discretion, and with
but few, if any, checks, very large sums of money;
and in the course of the late war he drew on the
Treasury for more than six hundred thousand dollars
for military purposes.   Yet General Harrison retired
from the public service poorer than he entered it,
and has never been a defaulter to his Government.
There are but two instances, it is believed, in which
even a whisper of suspicion against the purity of his
official conduct has been heard.   One of these, made
by an army contractor, was investigated in Congress,
and the charge triumphantly refuted.   The other
occurred while Governor of Indiana.   A foreigner
residing in that Territory, by the name of McIntosh,

and possessing very considerable wealth, having taken some offence, charged Governor Harrison with having defrauded the Indians in the treaty of Fort Wayne, made in the year 1809. The accused very properly concluded that it was due to his own reputation, not less than to the interests of the general Government, that a charge of this kind should be fully investigated in a court of justice. He, therefore, instituted a suit in the Supreme Court of the Territory, and, after a full and fair trial before a judge and jury of admitted impartiality between the parties, a verdict was rendered against the defendant for four thousand dollars. The evidence was so conclusive in favor of Governor Harrison, that McIntosh did not attempt to press the truth of the charge upon the jury, but only sought to lessen the amount of damages by pleading some matters in extenuation of his conduct. When the property of the defendant was levied upon to satisfy the judgment, it was bought in by an agent of the Governor, who immediately distributed one-third of it among the orphan children of his fellow-citizens that had died in battle ; and then restored the remainder to McIntosh himself. It has been well observed that 'no language of praise can add to the truth and force of the simple beauty of such an example of magnanimity, disinterestedness, and generosity.' Some years since it was discovered that a large tract of land, adjoining Cincinnati, which had been sold long previously for a very small sum, under an execution against the original proprietor of the Miami country, could not be held under this sale in consequence of some defective proceedings in court. The legal title to this tract, now immensely valuable, was vested in

10

Mrs. Harrison and another individual, as heirs-at-law. Immediately upon being informed of the situation of this property, General Harrison procured the consent of the co-heir, and joined him in releasing to the purchasers the whole of this land, without claiming any other consideration than the few hundred dollars which constituted the difference between the actual value at the time when sold, and the amount paid at the sheriff's sale. In 1804, the Governor of Indiana was, upon the suggestion of President Jefferson, made *ex-officio* Governor of 'Upper Louisiana.' Under the impression that it was sound policy to convince the inhabitants of the newly-acquired territory that they had lost nothing by the change, Governor Harrison declined receiving the fees he was entitled to by law, although those for Indian licenses alone would have brought him several thousand dollars. At the same time, the proprietor of St. Louis offered him, for a mere nominal sum, an undivided moiety of three-fourths of the town of St. Louis, and the adjoining lands, if he would assist in building up that place. Such, however, was his nice sense of honor, that he declined the offer, fearing it might be said that he had used his official station to promote his private interest. The property thus voluntarily refused, and which might have been accepted without any violation of principle, is probably worth at this time a million of dollars. While acting as Commander-in-Chief of the Northwestern army, General Harrison's expenses, owing to the extent of his command, and the amount of company he was obliged to entertain at headquarters, so far exceeded his pay, that he was compelled, before the close of the war, to sell a valuable tract of land to meet the current demands upon his purse. Soon after his resignation in the army, while the claims of a large family were pressing upon him, General Harrison had made up his mind to ask an appointment for one of his sons at West Point. Before the application was made, however, a poor boy, the child of a neighbor, who had not the means of obtaining an education, made a personal appeal to the General to procure him a place in this institution. He immediately waived the claims of his own son, and obtained a warrant for this poor lad, who was educated at the academy, and is now a distinguished citizen of Indiana, and takes great pleasure in bearing testimony to the noble disinterestedness of his patron. Similar instances of integrity and generosity might be multiplied, had we further space to narrate the incidents in the life of the veteran, whose patriotic policy founded, and whose skilful valor defended, the vast Northwest. The literary talent and attainment of General Harrison are uncommonly good. He is a sound scholar, not only familiar with the passing literature of the day, but possessing a familiar acquaintance with ancient history, especially with the classic annals of Greece and Rome. His own writings and conversation are forcibly illustrated by allusions to these works, and frequently bear evidence of a mind richly imbued with the philosophy of history. The productions of his pen, which are thrown off without an effort, are at once smooth, strong, and perspicuous, and written with remarkable simplicity and beauty of style. As a speaker, he is animated, fluent, and forcible; correct in his language, and peculiarly ready in bringing the resources of a cultivated understanding to bear upon any given subject. Both in body and mind, General Harrison enjoys a 'green old age.' His step is firm, his spirits buoyant, his conversation sprightly, instructive, and rich in anecdote. His countenance is expressive of kindness and genuine philanthropy; and his dark, piercing eye has lost little, if any, of the fire and vivacity of his more youthful days. The strength of his memory and the accuracy of his judgment remain unimpaired. One of the latest productions of his pen, written but a few weeks since, is strongly characterized by the force, raciness, and nice discrimination, which belong to the meridian of his life. In temperament, warm and impulsive ; in manners, plain and unassuming ; in his habits, generous and hospitable, General Harrison combines, in an eminent degree, the manly frankness of a soldier, with the sturdy independence of a farmer."

The campaign closed in a blaze of glory. Harrison was elected by one of the largest majorities ever given to any President. He was very popular with the people of the West, many of whom to this day love to recall around their hearthstones the incidents of that famous campaign. The terms *Log Cabin* and *Hard Cider*, which were inscribed upon the Whig banners, transparencies, etc., originated in this way. General Harrison's house at North Bend, Ohio, or at least a part of it, was one of the original log cabins built by the early settlers of that country, and covered with clap-boards. The story became current that the great chieftain lived in the plainest manner in his log cabin, and that his latch-string was always hung on the outside, and that the humblest man in the country could enter whenever he pleased, and would always find a hearty welcome and a mug of cider ready for him. General Harrison was a very temperate man, and said, I think, in one of his speeches, that the strongest liquor he ever drank was a mug of hard cider. Anyhow, the story became popular, and pictures representing a log cabin and barrels of cider were emblazoned on the banners and transparencies of the Whigs, which were carried triumphantly in their processions, in the midst of the wildest cheers, in which all classes joined, the high and low, and rich and poor.

It is no exaggeration to say that more than a thousand and one songs were written in praise of the log cabin and "Old Tippecanoe," as Harrison was familiarly called.

The following is a verse from one of the songs which any number of persons now living have helped to sing, or had dinned in their ears:

> "Hurrah for the Log Cabin, chief of our choice!
>   For the Old Indian Fighter, hurrah!
> Hurrah! and from mountain to valley the voice
>   Of the people re-echoes hurrah!
> Then come to the ballot-box, boys! Come along!
>   He never lost battle for you;
> Let us down with oppression and tyranny's throng,
>   And up with Old Tippecanoe!"

CHAPTER VII.

General Harrison expresses his Gratitude for Colonel Todd's Services —
His Appointment as Minister to Russia — Success of his Mission —
Felicitous Speech of Colonel Todd at a Banquet in St. Petersburg —
Motley and Maxwell in his Official Family — Colonel Todd's Visit to
the Interior of Russia — Important Despatches.

GENERAL HARRISON was very grateful for the services Colonel Todd rendered him during the campaign. And he often said that he owed, in a great part, his triumph to him, and on one occasion, while discussing with his Cabinet the appointments and duties of the administration, said to Mr. Webster: "I shall not be satisfied with the appointments of the Department of State, unless a first-class position is given to my old friend and companion-in-arms, Colonel Todd." As an instance of the regard in which Colonel Todd was held by General Harrison's family, it may be added, that, when General Harrison was taking leave of his family for his inauguration at Washington, Mrs. Harrison, putting her arms around him, exclaimed: "*General, I want you to take care of our dear friend, Colonel Todd; he loves you so much.*" Colonel Todd accompanied General Harrison to Washington, and remained with him as a member of his family during the short interval that he occupied the Presidential chair; and, as the last sad office, accompanied his remains to North Bend, and, by request of Mrs. Harrison, selected the spot for his burial.

On the death of Harrison, President Tyler, desiring to carry out the wishes of Harrison, appointed

Colonel Todd envoy - extraordinary to St. Petersburg. While in Russia, Colonel Todd elicited the
most flattering compliments from the Administration.
Mr. Webster was particularly lavish in the praise he
bestowed on him. The Emperor of Russia showed
him many marks of his esteem, and would have him
attend his parades, where often more than one hundred and fifty thousand troops exhibited their skill
and discipline. Colonel Todd induced the Emperor
to secure the services of the distinguished engineer,
Mr. Whistler, for the construction of railroads in the
empire. Colonel Todd was elected a member of the
Imperial Agricultural Society, which is the only com-
pliment of the kind, I believe, that has ever been paid
to an American citizen. Colonel Todd was one of the
best speakers at a banquet I ever heard. After-din-
ner speeches are seldom readable, on account of the
subjects which present themselves being so hack-
neyed that it is almost impossible for a speaker to
say anything new in reference to them.

The following speech of Colonel Todd's, delivered
at the celebration of the English Diplomatic Club, is,
I think, wholly free from objections of this kind. It
was extensively copied by the English and American
papers, and Mr. Webster spoke of it as being in
very fine taste. The President of the Club, Count
Worontzord Daschhoff, after having proposed the
health of the Emperor, offered a toast to the nations
in unity with Russia. Colonel Todd then said:

"I rise to address the President with mingled emotions of pleasure and regret,—pleasure, for the com-
pliment you have conferred in asking me to respond

to the toast to the nations in unity with Russia ; and regret, on beholding the vacant chair of Baron Sleglitz, whose animated eyes gave evidence a year ago of the delight he enjoyed in this anniversary. He was the Rothschild of Russia. If there are any Englishmen here, I thank them in the name of the descendants of those Englishmen who first planted a government of laws in Massachusetts and in Virginia, the mother of nearly all the American Presidents. I congratulate England and America on the recent treaty that has reconciled their principal difficulty. This treaty will give new vigor to their commercial relations. I congratulate them on being preserved from war, which, in its progress, might have involved even gigantic Russia, whose colossal arms reach over Europe, Asia, and America. May England and America be rivals only in the race for true glory.

"If there are any Swedes here, I thank them in the name of the descendants of those that first civilized New Jersey, whose gallant and intellectual sons render her worthy of such worthy sires. If there are any Frenchmen here, I thank them in the name of the descendants of the Huguenots, who fled from the Old World after the revolution of the Edict of Nantes, and formed a home in the New World, and imparted their noble character to South Carolina, the Palmetto State of the South.

"If there are any Dutchmen here, I thank them in the name of the descendants of those Hollanders who first peopled the Empire State, New York ; one of whose sons, *Washington Irving*, now adorns the American Diplomatic service as Minister to Spain, and delights all Europe with sketches of England —

enlightened, free, and *powerful* England, who would place his name to the remotest posterity in the same wreath of fame that encircles the brow of her own Addison.

"If there are any Germans here, I thank them in the name of their German brethren in Pennsylvania, and Ohio, and of the beautiful city of Cincinnati, which, in respect to the mechanic arts, internal trade, architectural taste, and noble institutions of literature and benevolence, may be justly regarded as the Moscow of the New World. If there are any Russians here, I thank them in the name of my forefathers, who were indebted to the friendship of the great Catharine in the Armed neutrality of 1780. I thank them in the name of my compatriots of 1814, who were under obligations to the liberal views and good offices of the Emperor Alexander of glorious memory.

"It is indeed a delightful task, to dwell upon the relation existing between Russia and the United States. It is something worthy of the contemplation of other Powers, to see two great nations, the most extensive in territory and resources in the Old and the New World, always living in peace.

"Ancient and modern history present no such bright examples. To Russia and America the temple of Janus has ever been closed. May it never be opened. I conclude with offering an apology for having probably exhausted your patience. When my beloved country is complimented in a foreign land, my heart is full, and out of the fulness of the heart the mouth speaketh. I propose the health of the hereditary Grand - Duke. May he emulate in his career the destiny which his august father has ful-

11

filled in combining the energy of Peter with the magnanimity of Alexander."

At the time Colonel Todd was appointed to the
embassy at Russia, John Lathrop Motley was chosen
the First Secretary of Legation.   Mr. Motley had
travelled in Europe, and had passed a year at the
University of Göttingen, and a year at Berlin, and he
proved a delightful companion and a warm personal
friend of Colonel Todd's.   Motley had published, the
year previous, a very interesting novel, entitled *Mor-
ton's Hope, or the Memoirs of a Young Provincial,* and he
was anxious to make himself thoroughly acquainted
with Russia and the Russians, for the purpose of writing a book on the subject.   The salary of the Secretary
of Legation at St. Petersburg is very small, and
Mr. Motley was not able to support his family with
it; and, after a short residence there of about two
months, he returned to the United States; but during
that short time he became so well acquainted with
the customs of the country, that he was enabled to
prepare one of the most valuable essays on Peter the
Great that has ever been written.

Mr. Maxwell, another able and accomplished author,
was appointed to the place vacated by Mr. Motley.
Mr. Maxwell accompanied Colonel Todd to the interior of Russia during the great fair at Nishnei Novo-
grodek.

This was the first instance of an American Minister
ever having penetrated into the interior of the Empire further than Moscow; and Colonel Todd gave a
highly interesting account of the trip in a despatch
to the State Department.   Colonel Todd mentioned,

that, after having secured the necessary passport, he set out from St. Petersburg on the 18th of August, and extended his journey as far as Nishnei, at the junction of the Oka with the Volga, and from thence to Kazan, the ancient Tartar capital, situated a short distance above the mouth of the Kama. If he had travelled two days further, he would have reached the western limits of Asia. I have often heard Colonel Todd speak of the pains he took to interest the people on his route in America, and to encourage among them a friendly feeling toward us. Colonel Todd also witnessed the terrible conflagration at Kazan, which destroyed more than two-thirds of the entire city. This was one of the most extensive fires in the world, equalled probably only by the recent conflagration at Chicago. Colonel Todd, in one of his descriptions of the annual fair at Nishnei, said that more than three hundred thousand strangers had gathered there from all parts of the world. He said that it was a rare spectacle to see so many people speaking so many different languages. I remember his telling me how much interested he was in seeing in the interior of Russia the cotton and rice from our own country by the side of that grown in Bukaria.

Colonel Todd's despatches to the Secretary of State while at Russia are very interesting and instructive. In his letters to M. Bodisco and Count Nesselrode he showed how utterly impossible it was for him to allow anything to escape his attention that concerned the interest of the United States. The following despatch, in reference to our commerce with Russia, addressed to that accomplished scholar and diplomatist, Count Nesselrode, explains itself:

"THE UNITED STATES LEGATION AT ST. PETERSBURG.

" The undersigned pays his respect, etc., to his Excellency Count Nesselrode, the Chancellor of the Empire, and
has the honor to acknowledge the receipt of his Excellency's
note of the 23d June (O. S.), together with its enclosure,
consisting of a despatch of that date to his Excellency M.
Bodisco, his Imperial Majesty's Minister Plenipotentiary at
Washington, which his Excellency the Chancellor is pleased
to regard as a full reply to the note of the undersigned of
12th June, '24, in relation to the right of the United States
to participate in the recent favor granted to English commerce.

" The undersigned regrets to perceive, from the general
tenor of that despatch, an unwillingness on the part of the
Imperial Ministry to extend the favor to the United States.
He the more regrets the result from the special ground on
which his Excellency the Chancellor has predicated the opinion that the United States cannot, in this case, insist upon the
application of the stipulations of the thirteenth article of the
existing treaty between Russia and the United States ; his
Excellency asserting the right of the Imperial Government
to deny this privilege to the United States upon the plea
that the concession to England was not gratuitous, but
was a part return for certain reductions in the tariff of her
Britannic Majesty favorable to Russian exports.

" The undersigned, in adverting to the admission made
by his Excellency in the recent interview, that this favor
was without condition, does not doubt that his Excellency
had reference in that remark to the terms of the Ukase,
containing, as it does, no allusion to the modifications in
the English tariff. The undersigned, however, did not understand his Excellency as maintaining in that interview,
nor in the despatch to M. Bodisco, that these British modifications were avowed by that Government to be conditional upon the fact of his Majesty's Government adopting
equivalent regulations in favor of Great Britain. On the

contrary, the undersigned supposes that these changes in the English tariff were made without cor-litions; for if they had been made conditional, he presumes, the Ukase would have contained a reference to such conditions in addition to the other motives stated in that document. In the absence, then, of such conditions upon the face of the Imperial Ukase, or of the contingency supposed that the British regulations were not conditional, the undersigned deems it due to the interest of his country, designed to be secured by the thirteenth article of the existing treaty, not to admit the soundness of the position which his Excellency has advanced in the despatch to M. Bodisco. He is equally at a loss to perceive the 'applicability of the suggestion that the exports of Russia to the United States do not find a ready sale in consequence of the heavy duties in the American tariff. No treaty, or public law, prevents either nation from regulating its duties on imports in such mode as to it may seem right and proper. In the exercise of this right, the United States have only sanctioned the principle and practice of Russia in similar cases. Both nations desire, very justly, to protect their own industry; and if the United States, by a protective duty, are making progress in securing even a partial supply at home of hemp and its fabrics, his Majesty's Government has exercised a similar right in the heavy duties upon tobacco, amounting to a prohibition in the direct trade. The right to impose countervailing duties is admitted as belonging to both nations. But the undersigned cannot perceive the propriety of the Imperial Ministry treating the duties on Russian products in the United States as authority for granting a special favor to England, which, upon its face, is without conditions, but which is attempted by subsequent explanations to be regarded as conditions, and therefore not subject to the stipulations of the thirteenth article of the existing treaty. His Excellency the Chancellor has suggested that this favor to England is an experiment for this season, made with the design to foster the native industry of Russia in the establishments for refining sugars; and that it is, therefore, impracticable to enter into negotiations on this subject, until there shall be time afforded to test the result of the experiment. The undersigned cannot suppose it was the intention of his Excellency to advance the opinion that a favor granted to England does not enure to the benefit of the United States, under the thirteenth article of the existing treaty, merely because it is an experiment for this season of navigation; nor does he suppose that the recent changes in the English tariff are designed only as an experiment for this season. On the contrary, he supposes that, if they were made permanent without reference to a repeal at any specified time, the favor to England must become permanent, and thus this ground for delay in extending the favor to the United States during this season looses the force which his Excellency the Chancellor has been pleased to attach to it.

"The undersigned repeats his solicitude to be able to transmit to his Government an answer to his note of the 12th of June, O. S., of a character more favorable to American interest than that contained in the despatch to M. Bodisco; for he is aware that the season for navigation is passing away too rapidly to expect that any shipments can be made during this year from America, if they are to depend upon the result of explanations between his Excellency M. Bodisco and the Department of State at Washington.

"In the hope that the Imperial Ministry may, upon a review of this subject, extend to the United States the favor already granted to England, the undersigned avails himself of the occasion to renew to his Excellency the Chancellor an assurance of his perfect respect.

C. S. TODD."

"18th July, 1845."

The despatch of Colonel Todd to M. Bodisco, in June, 1845, as to the importation of crushed sugar, is a very valuable document, and may appropriately be introduced here:

" Your Excellency is aware that the manufacture of sugar from the cane has, for a number of years, formed a branch of industry with us, which our commercial legislation always protects. From a regard to the interests of our native refineries, raw sugar alone is allowed to enter by the tariff; and all sugar of the cane which has passed through any degree of purification, excluded. This system has been maintained until now. The disasters suffered during the past year by the plantations of Cuba, however, have led the Imperial Government to consider the means that may be necessary to prevent too great a rise in the price of sugar ; and, by the Ukase of 19th of March, the importation of sugar half refined, bruised, or in lumps, commonly called (in commerce) *crushed lumps*, has been allowed. At the same time, in order to protect native manufactures, they are admitted only under certain restrictions ; they must be imported for the use of refineries alone, and pay the same duties as raw sugar, viz., *three roubles, eighty copitcs, silver, per pound.* The importation, furthermore, is limited to the harbor of St. Petersburg and to the duration of the navigation of 1845. Besides, even this temporary admission has not been generally granted, but is confined to the sugar lumps coming from England. Aside from the interests of our refineries, this last arrangement has been induced by the steps taken on the part of the British Government for several years past, to obtain for English commerce the right of importing lumps, but especially by the facilities and marked deductions of duties which the new English tariff offers to Russian commerce.

" The preference conceded to England, though but temporary, seems to have alarmed the American commerce. The United States Minister has come to converse with me on the subject; citing, among others, the stipulations of the treaty of 6-18th December, 1832, which assures to American commerce in Russia the same rights and privileges enjoyed by the most favored nations. I have hastened to present to Mr. Todd the explanations best suited to exhibit the nature and object of the arrangements in question. Not only are they provisory and adopted as a simple experiment, but they do not seem to us to be opposed to the stipulations of the treaty cited by Mr. Todd.

"These stipulations have never been lost sight of. On the contrary, we think they have been constantly and scrupulously observed. American commerce has always met with the most favorable treatment from us, and the principle of reciprocity consecrated in the treaty has never experienced, and could never experience, the slightest infraction at our hands. But the eleventh article of the treaty reserves to us expressly the right of granting to other nations any special favor in point of commerce and navigation, provided this favor be made common to the United States, and the latter enjoy it gratuitously, if the concession be gratuitous, or by means of the same compensations, if conditional.

"Now the admission of crushed lumps coming from England has not been gratuitously conceded. It is, as already said, a just return for the arrangement of the new English tariff. The Imperial Government has, therefore, thought itself justified in making this concession to England, with the reserve, if need be, of having an understanding with the Government of the United States on the conditions under which the American commerce could be admitted to participate in the same. Even now would we be ready to enter into negotiations on this matter, if, as observed above, the arrangement concerning crushed lumps were not a temporary and provisory measure.

"The year 1845 will, doubtless, be sufficient to show how far it will be necessary to prolong the duration or extend the application of this measure. Experience alone, however, will be able to influence the Imperial Government in deciding on this matter. Yet, if, without too great injury to native industry, the possibility of admitting conditionally half-refined sugars should be thereby demonstrated, the Russian Government would not fail to take into due consideration the interest and wishes of American commerce. The Government of the United States, on the other hand, will no doubt lend its aid to facilitate the realization of these friendly arrangements, manifesting, in return, due regard to the interests of Russian commerce, and the wishes that might be expressed by us.

" Too heavy duties are imposed on several Russian products in the United States to allow of their being sold with any advantage there. A reduction of duties on these objects would, therefore, take away one of the obstacles which still hinder the entire development of commercial relations between the two countries.

" I 'invite you, Sir, to make explanations in this sense to the Cabinet at Washington."

12

CHAPTER VIII.

Colonel Todd returns to Frankfort — Delivers a Lecture on Russia —
Withdraws from a Contest for the Governorship of Kentucky — Accepts
the Office of Commissioner under the Mexican Treaty — Advocates a
Railroad to the Pacific.

COLONEL TODD'S mission to Russia expired
in 1846, and he returned to the·United States,
and resumed the practice of law at Frankfort, Ky.
A short time after his return he was invited to deliver
a lecture before the Frankfort *Athenæum*, on the
Russian Empire.

The lecture may be appropriately introduced here
entire. It is one of the best condensed accounts
that I have ever read concerning that empire:

"RUSSIA: HER RESOURCES, RELIGION, LITERATURE, ETC.

"The Empire of Russia, in her vast extent and resources,
in her history and distinctive character, is new to us, as she
is indeed to many of the nations of the Old World. She
reaches from the Frozen Ocean to the Black Sea, and from
the Baltic and Gulf of Bothnia to the Ural Mountains, sep-
arating Europe from Asia, and thence through Siberia to
the Indian Ocean. She exceeds in territory all the nations
of Europe. Throughout her vast extent, with the exception
of the Ural Mountains, she presents one continuous plain,
embracing every variety of climate and production, with a
soil so rich and diversified that hemp, and many of the
tropical fruits, and nearly every species of grain, except
Indian corn, may be found among her exports.

"In considering this subject, I may be led to speak very
briefly of her history, religion, sciences, fine arts, literature,

commerce, agriculture, manufactures, revenue, debt, exports, navy, army, climate, nobility, merchants, and peasants; resources, government, police, and Emperor. The
most cursory examination of these various aspects of the
subject would alone fill a volume. It is my present purpose
to give them only a passing glance.

"*Of her History.* — Prior to the time of Peter the Great,
who assumed the title of Autocrat and Emperor, with absolute power, the ancient dynasty resided at Moscow under
the title of Grand-Duke or Czar, with princes of the Grand
Duchy exercising regal powers in the different governments or provinces, somewhat on the plan of the petty
sovereignties in Germany. At a very remote period, all
of the country beyond Poland was under the Tartar authority, with their capital at Kazan on the Volga, seven
hundred miles beyond Moscow. The religion of that
day was Mohammedan, and it was not until some eight
hundred years ago that the Greek religion was introduced
into Russia by the baptism of the Grand-Duchess Olga,
at Constantinople. Peter, by the establishment of his
capital on the Baltic, brought his nation, made up of many
tribes, into contiguity with Europe, and Russia thus ceased
to be an Asiatic power. Karamzin, her great historian,
has described, and Poushkin, her great poet, has sung the
ancient heroes of the country; but the story of Russia
is little known beyond the days of her first great law-
givers in the persons of Ivan and Alexis. Napoleon, on
witnessing, as he advanced into Russia, the destruction of
her resources and the burning of her ancient capital by the
self-sacrificing patriotism of her own subjects, affected to
speak of them as the modern Scythians; but, at this day,
the memory of Rostopchin, the governor of Moscow, is
regarded with the veneration due to a national benefactor.
Catharine the Second endeavored to carry out the system
of Peter, and rendered our patriotic fathers noble service
by her armed neutrality of 1780; and, in the war of 1812,
the enlightened Alexander placed our country under last-

ing obligation by the offer of his mediation with Great
Britain. While we were struggling as Colonies, the great
Peter was founding his city of palaces, and bringing Eastern magnificence into contact with the energy and arts of
Europe. Yet it is a memorable coincidence, that, when
Peter, the great Northern light, descended below the horizon
in 1725, Washington, the bright star of the West, arose in
1732, to become also the founder of a great nation, and to
present to distant ages 'an immortal example of true glory'
destined to 'shine on, like the path of the just, more and
more into the perfect day.'

" The best history of Russia is that by Karamzin, brought
up to the close of Alexander's reign. Interesting histories
of the War with Napoleon have been written by Bowtourlin
and Danilefsky. Bell's history is chiefly an epitome of
Karamzin. The most impartial account of travels in that
empire is by Elliott, an Englishman; also, in Letters from
the Baltic, by an English lady; in Travels by Kohl, a German ; and in Lectures by our excellent Dr. Baird.

" The Greek is the religion of Russia. Of the sixty
millions of subjects, upwards of forty millions are of the
national faith. The Emperor stands in the same relation
to the Greek that the Pope does to the Romish Church.
Until Peter assumed to himself all ecclesiastical as well as
political power, the head of the Church was called the
Patriarch, with archimandrites, metropolitans, and bishops.
I refer to an article published in the *Presbyterian Herald*, at
Louisville, about the first of January last, as showing a
comparison between the doctrines held in the Eastern or
Greek, and the Western or Romish Church. All Protestants
will recognize the Greek articles as according more nearly
with their own ; while the Emperor treats the Romish as
not orthodox. The forms in the Greek services are even
more imposing than those in the Romish, and the feast-
days are equally numerous. The period of Lent is kept
with great strictness, especially during the first and last
week. The festivities in the Carnival are very boisterous.

The ceremonies on Easter morning are peculiar, and par-
take largely of the courtesy belonging to Eastern manners.
To be a witness of five hundred Russian men kissing each
other in the streets on that day might perhaps be a compensation to some tastes for a trip to that distant region.
There are no seats in a Greek church; all the worshippers
stand up, and, during particular parts of the service by the
priests, the people cross themselves and bow, which is repeated from time to time when some more solemn occasion
leads them to kneel down and place their foreheads on the
floor. They are coming in and going out during the two
hours' service. None but vocal music is employed, and
this is rendered solemn and touching from a choir of twenty
or thirty boys from eight to twenty years of age; each
chanting one note. The priest usually reads with his back
to the congregation, and the service is performed inside of
a partition of lattice-work, perhaps like the inner veil of the
Temple. While the Emperor is jealous of proselytes being
made from his own Church, and all officers under the Government are required to take the sacrament once a year
in some church, his policy is above all praise in allowing
freedom of conscience and of public worship by every sect,
Catholics, Jews, Mohammedans, and Protestants; and it is
a fact creditable to the liberality of a monarch possessing unlimited power in Church and State, that, during my
residence in Russia, four, if not more, of his principal min-
isters — General Count Clein Michel, Minister of Ways and
Communications; Count Cancrire, Minister of Finance;
Count Nesselrode, Chancellor of the Empire and Secretary
of Foreign Affairs; and General Count Benkendorf, Chief
of the Military Staff and of the Secret Police — were all
Protestants, and among the ablest men in his Cabinet.

"The institutions for the promotion of science are entitled to high commendation. The records of the Imperial
Academy of Sciences show a valuable addition to the
department of universal knowledge. Their researches, by
land and by sea, are worthy of a place by the side of those

prosecuted by Great Britain, France, and America. The observatory, near St. Petersburg, is an honor to the Imperial taste, and contains the largest telescope in the world. It was manufactured at Munich, in Bavaria. The Museum connected with the Academy of Sciences is admirably arranged, with choice specimens from every quarter of the globe; among them the remains of the Mammoth found sixty years ago on the ice in the River Lena, the Mississippi of Siberia. The Imperial Botanical Garden is a proud monument of the public taste for this interesting science. The plants occupy a space of three-quarters of a mile, and have been collected, at vast expense, from every climate of the globe. Rich contributions have been made from Brazil, the Cape of Good Hope; from Australia, and from the Himalaya Mountains in Asia. A visitor to this great panorama of nature will be gratified by an inspection of the green and black tea trees of China, of all the acacias of the East, of all the fruit-trees of the tropics, and even the cane of the Mississippi. The collection would be unrivalled, if it had that most magnificent of evergreens, our own noble magnolia. The Imperial Library contains four hundred thousand volumes and twenty thousand manuscripts, among them a letter from Washington, whom they regard as the American Peter.

"The system of Public Instruction is entrusted to a minister of state. There are five universities in the Empire: at St. Petersburg, Moscow, Kazan, on the Volga, Keif, near the Black Sea, and at Dorpat, near Riga, on the Baltic. The colleges for boys, and institutes for girls, are sustained on the most liberal plan. There is a college connected with the Foreign Office, in which those destined for the diplomatic service are taught the Asiatic languages. It is this system, and their aptitude to acquire foreign languages, that gives such efficiency to the representatives of the Empire abroad. The edifice devoted to the Academy of Fine Arts conveys a just impression of the public taste; it contains a rich collection, not only of foreign and ancient paintings, but many

of great merit by native artists.   The Russians are distinguished as copyists.   Their genius is particularly displayed
in the erection of the Bronze Horse; and the Equestrian
Statue of Peter, in the St. Isaac's Square, is the most celebrated effort of the kind in Europe.   The collection of
paintings in the Hermitage, connected with the winter
palace, claims the attention of the traveller as much as the
collections at Berlin, Dresden, Versailles, and the Louvre.

" The Imperial Arsenal, at Tsarsko-Celo, is a remarkable
curiosity; the armor of the last six centuries is there displayed; the object of deepest interest in the collection
being the celebrated Tippoo-Saib sitting upon the stuffed
skin of his identical war-horse, the most perfect model of
that animal extant.

"In touching briefly upon the Fine Arts, I may add that
too much praise cannot be awarded to Peter the Great, for
inculcating among his subjects, by his own noble example,
the importance of the mechanic arts to the welfare of a
State.   He visited Holland, to study the trade of a ship-
builder; and I saw, near the church of the Ancient For-
tress, where the remains of the Imperial family are deposited,
and near the Mint, in which the precious metals of Siberia
are coined, the first boat which that great artist constructed,
and with which he navigated the Baltic.   This practical
knowledge became the means of several victories over the
Turks, in which the Czar himself was the admiral.   I saw,
also, the first log cabin he had erected on the island where
the veneration of his' people has preserved the clothes and
the implements with which he followed the trade of a cob-
bler, presenting to his subjects the same brilliant contrast
of public usefulness to the lazy career of the nobility, which
the great Roger Sherman (the shoemaker of Connecticut)
exhibited to the aristocracy of our own country.   But it
should be borne in mind, that the handicraft specimens of
the great mechanic were only the trifles of his industry;
that these did not interfere with his gigantic energy, as a
statesman, in consolidating various tribes into one govern-

ment, and in giving character and nationality to the whole mass of what were then his barbarous subjects; nor did his enlightened plans of policy arrest his efforts, by skill and valor in the field, to fortify his dynasty against the invasion by Charles XII. of Sweden.

"The Literature of Russia deserves more respect than the journals of other nations have assigned to it. In the departments of history, of science, of poetry, and of diplomacy, she should rank with many nations claiming to be more civilized. The language resembles the Greek in sound, having six Greek letters in the alphabet. Their historians have been already named; Lomonosoff, Kautemar, Derjavine, Poushkin, and Koukolnic, will compare with the poets of ancient or modern times; while the fame of Romanozoff, Lieven, Matenzervic, and Nesselrode will descend to posterity in the same diplomatic wreath with that of Talleyrand, Metternich, and Castlereagh, and only equalled by the ability that has distinguished the State papers of our own loved land.

"The Commerce of Russia is chiefly internal and continental, especially in the interchange of products with China and the East Indies. The vast canals, commenced by Peter, have been completed by his successors; and there is now an internal communication between the Baltic and the Caspian Sea, independently of canals in Siberia that lead to rivers emptying into that great inland lake. Along this route the coarse cloths of Russia find their way to Kiatka, on the frontier of China, and the famous tea of the East, grown only in the northern districts and never exported by sea, is brought to the Caspian, and thence up the Volga to the great annual fair at Nishnai, Novogorod, and thence by that river and canals to St. Petersburg. This voyage is effected in two years, owing to the long winter blocking up the canals. The foreign commerce is carried on from St. Petersburg and Riga on the Baltic, and from Odessa and Tangarog on the Black Sea. I deem it unnecessary, in this place, to speak of the extent of this foreign commerce, being content to allude only to the character of her import duties; these are eminently protective upon all the articles entering into competition with her manufactures, and are, in some instances, prohibitory, as in the case of the direct introduction of our tobacco, while our cotton is scarcely burdened with any duty. A recent Ukase, permitting the introduction of crushed sugars from England, has nearly destroyed the indirect trade so profitable to our navigating interests, in which we send the Havana sugars to Russia. It is a source of satisfaction, however, to know that the manufacturing establishments in that Empire are inducing a fourfold increase in the consumption of our cotton.

" The Agriculture of Russia has not advanced as rapidly as her other branches of national industry, notwithstanding the Emperor is aided by the enlightened labors of an agricultural society, of which I had the honor to be elected a member. A laudable spirit, however, is just waking up there, as elsewhere, to advance this greatest of national interests. The implements of husbandry, in the interior, are of the rudest kind, though the cheapness of labor enables the cultivator to prepare his lands in a mode much neater than we should expect from the character of the implements. In this respect, a happy change is taking place in the desire to procure from America the improvements that distinguish our genius and energy, of which we have a gratifying evidence in the selection of a celebrated American engineer, Major Whistler, to superintend the railroad to Moscow, four hundred and forty miles, and the employment of Messrs. Harrison and Eastwick and Winans to construct the locomotives and cars — a proud monument to American genius, skill, and integrity. Indeed, all the valuable inventions of our country are sought for, except our greatest invention, that of a Representative Democracy. The Agricultural Society of Russia is beginning to exercise the wholesome influence of giving dignity to the profession. The Emperor often suggests plans for its consideration,

13

and adds valuable premiums for judicious improvements. Two of these plans were intimately connected with the national welfare : one, to procure an account of the most improved mode of kiln-drying grain, for exportation to the warm climates ; and the other, the most effectual scheme for preventing a scarcity of food in one province, while there should be a great supply in other provinces. This great desideratum is to be obtained solely by the construction of good roads, and other facilities of intercommunication, and is doubtless occupying at this time the sagacity and energy of her indefatigable sovereign. In travelling to the interior, I was struck with the practice, so little known among us, of women reaping in the harvest-fields, a practice so general on the continent, and which is even tolerated in intellectual Scotland. In Russia, as indeed throughout the continent of Europe, the fields are cultivated without division-fences,—the cattle and the sheep are attended by shepherds with their dogs, while the pigs are kept up in small lots near the dwelling. How different from the vast extent and care bestowed in our country upon fences to head that little animal !

"The Manufactures of Russia are beginning to elevate her in the estimation of other powers ; vast efforts are in progress to extend the manufacture of refined sugar, of glass, and of cotton, the latter of which is leading to a rapid increase in the introduction of our great staple. A few years ago we had only ten, now we have sixty large ships engaged in that trade. There are many large manufacturing establishments for sheet-iron, and cotton and woollen cloths, around Moscow ; an interesting establishment, at Tula, for the manufacture of fire-arms and cutlery ; and, in the district of Crimea, a large capital is employed in the manufacture of sugar from beets. At Moscow there is an annual fair for the exhibition of native manufactured articles ; and a fair for the exchange of Asiatic, European, and American products at Nijnel Novogorod, on the Volga, four hundred miles beyond Moscow. Two hundred thousand merchants, of different nations, are collected at the fair, and I could, in a two hours' walk along the respective streets, hear twenty different languages spoken.   It was here that I found the cotton of the Mississippi, and the rice of South Carolina, by the side of the cotton and rice of Bokhara in the East Indies, each brought six thousand miles to be exchanged in the centre of Russia ; and it was here, too, that I encountered the rare incident of being supplied at a Persian hotel with barbecued mutton, and with what we call a Barrett melon, grown from the seed of a melon cultivated at Astrachan, at the mouth of the Volga, on the Caspian Sea.

"The Revenue of Russia amounts to about one hundred million silver rubles, and is derived chiefly from the following sources, to wit:

	Silver Rubles.
Capitation tax on serfs	20,000,000
Tax on peasants (in lieu of personal service) . .	16,000,000
Customs for St. Petersburg (other parts not included)	15,868,904
Salt tax	14,500,000
Brandy tax	36,500,000
Stamps	2,000,000
Mints	2,105,000
Per cent. tax on merchants' capital	1,500,000
Tax on private mining in Siberia	2,000,000
218 poods of gold from Government mines in Siberia, at 12,000 silver rubles each pood . . .	2,616,000
Total	93,089,904

"The Debt, though large, is relatively small compared with her resources and with the debt and resources of other Continental powers; it is about three hundred million silver rubles, or two hundred and twenty - five million dollars, to which may be added the expenses of the railroad to Moscow at fifty million rubles.   The debt is a perpetual loan, subject to redemption at any time by the Government; and her credit is higher than that of any government in Europe.   The exports of the Empire consist

chiefly of wheat and rye, hemp and its fabrics, such as sail-
duck, cordage, &c., tallow, deal, &c.; and the large item of
tallow indicates that it is a fine grass country,—blue grass,
timothy, clover, and orchard grass being cultivated extensively and with great success. Oats, barley, and manna are
cultivated chiefly for home consumption. The Irish potato
is grown in abundance, and of a quality equal to that cultivated on the Island of Michilimackinac. On visiting Mars
Hill, near Moscow,— from whence Napoleon and his army
first saw the object of their toils and ambition, and from
whence I could have an entire view of that ancient city,
with her gorgeous churches and mosques, with her venerable Kremlin, with her undulating, winding streets, and her
magnificent edifices, partly Asiatic and partly European,— I
could but designate the valley for miles along the adjacent
river as a great cabbage patch; cabbage soup, rye bread,
and salt, being the general and national diet of the peasantry.

" The Navy of Russia, so far as ships are concerned,
ranks as the third, if not the second, among the powers of
Europe. It consists of nearly three hundred ships, many of
them eighty, and a few of one hundred and twenty, guns.
These are employed chiefly in the Baltic and Black seas;
the want, however, of a great commercial marine must limit
the efficiency of these heavy floating batteries. The Emperor manifests a laudable ambition in his efforts to increase
this arm of his power. He is multiplying the number of
his war-steamers, and thinks the day is not far distant when
these will supersede, in some degree, the use of the line-of-
battle ships. The ' Kamschatska,' built by his authority at
New York, is decidedly the finest war-steamer in Europe,
being second only to our own ' Missouri' burned at Gibraltar.
The voyages of Kruzenstern, written in masterly style, do
honor to the enterprise of Russia; and this venerable admiral permitted me to witness the exercises of the naval
cadets under his care, where my national pride was gratified
by seeing a model of our late frigate ' President' used in

their naval lectures.   The naval character of Russia was
well sustained by Peter, as her admiral in the Black Sea,
and subsequently by Potemkin in the reign of Catherine,
and more recently by Admiral Heyden, who commanded
her fleet in the battle of Navarino.

" The Army of Russia exceeds in numbers that of any
power in Europe.   The regular force, which, in 1841, was
nearly one million, has been reduced to seven hundred
thousand ; of these, one hundred to one hundred and fifty
thousand are employed on the frontier of the Caucasus ;
fifty thousand constitute the Imperial Guard at St. Petersburg, and the rest are stationed among the interior governments 'of this vast Empire.   The Emperor readily avails
himself of the improvements introduced into other countries in the equipments of this his great hobby, and it appears to be an object of great solicitude to keep pace with
the condition of the French troops.   The army is recruited
from time to time, according to the Emperor's opinion of
the public exigencies, by a requisition upon the nobility for
a certain per cent., from the peasantry, and such an amount
as he may choose to raise from the Crown peasants.   Military colonies are maintained in the interior, particularly
in the direction of the Black Sea, where the soldiers are
exercised in the winter and assist their families during the
summer in the cultivation of the Crown lands.   For mus-
cular energy and intelligence, the Russian soldiers do not
compare favorably with the French or American ; but in
the precision of the military movements, especially on
parade, they are superior to any other troops.   Their firmness and constancy under a murderous fire have been at-
tested on many of the best fought fields in Europe, whether
under Suwarrow in Italy, or Benningsen and Platoff in
Germany, or Kutosof and Barclay de Tolly.   No adequate
conception can be formed, in this country, of the brilliancy
of an Imperial review of St. Petersburg, or of the interesting
manœuvres of fifty to one hundred thousand regulars at the
summer encampment.   The army, in two opposing divi-

sions, executes all the supposed operations of a real campaign. To these exercises I was always invited by the
Emperor; and, during 1845, witnessed the combination of
one hundred thousand men, of which twenty thousand were
cavalry, each regiment with a different major and horses of
different colors, though each horse, in a regiment, was
precisely alike. These horses are taught to move, at the
sound of music, from a walk to a trot, then to a gallop, and
thence back to a walk, always marking time. I should
scarcely venture to state these facts, if some visitor to St.
Petersburg had not published a similar account.

"I beg leave, in this place, to read an extract from my
Despatch No. 61, addressed to the Department of State, in
September, 1845, in which my views as to the value of
flying artillery, and suggestions as to our naval force, were
placed in the possession of our Government before the
commencement of the present war with Mexico: 'I add a
copy of sundry notes from Aid-de-camp-General Count Or-
luff, inviting me to the military review during the months of
June, July, and August, in which one hundred thousand troops
were engaged. Prince Charles of Russia and the brother of
the King of Holland, who married a sister of the Empress,
attended these reviews. It was a gratifying spectacle to
witness, as I did, from an eminence, a line of troops extending two miles on my right and an equal distance on my
left, in a plain so level that I could see the smoke of the
artillery upon each of the distant flanks, and the exercises
were closed by a magnificent display in three columns, one
of seventy-five thousand infantry, a battalion deep, and
extending more than a mile; another of two hundred pieces
of artillery; and the other, of twenty thousand cavalry of
twenty-five regiments, each with a different uniform and
horses of different colors, though the horses of the same
regiment were precisely alike. I was impressed by the
richness of the uniforms of the cavalry regiments, as well as
by the action and discipline of the horses; by the remarkable precision with which the infantry moved; and, most

of all, by the celerity with which the flying artillery was managed. It was this new arm, followed by the combinations and rapid concentrations of an adept, which gave to Napoleon his superiority over the tactics of the great Frederick; and although, in a defensive war, it may not be so valuable to us, the plains of Texas, Oregon, California, or Mexico, may present a theatre for its successful application in our service. The corps of Cossacks, both of the Don and of the Black Sea, so formidable to the retreating French in the invasion of 1812, as well as a small battalion of Circassians, excited a peculiar interest from their skilful use of the lance by the one, and the adroit horsemanship and practised gunnery of the other at half speed, so like the mounted riflemen of our great Western Valley. It struck me as a very judicious plan, to attach a squadron of lancers to each park of flying artillery, and the whole scene afforded evidence of the vast superiority which discipline gives over mere valor, in all cases where the local position and natural defences do not impart to raw troops the confidence which discipline alone inspires.

"'I have pleasure in noticing frequent allusion in the St. Petersburg Journal, published under the eye of this Government, to our country as a great maritime power. It is this impression which is best calculated to insure a respect for our rights; and perhaps no disposition of the steamer *Mississippi*, and of the *Pennsylvania*, would be more judicious than to show them to the Emperor, whose estimate of our capacity, of our power, is chiefly regulated by his conviction of our ability to contend for the freedom of the seas, of which Great Britain arrogantly assumes to be the mistress. I trust you will pardon me for this suggestion upon subjects strictly military and naval; but when we look at the unauthorized efforts of leading European papers to control the action of independent American States, we cannot avoid examining the means by which all European interference with the affairs of the New World shall be rebuked.'

"The Climate of Russia was to me a subject of much

misconception, before my arrival in that country; I found
the winters to agree with my constitution, and my health
throughout was firmer than at any period of my life. The
cold season commences early in October, and often continues until the first of May. I crossed the Neva in a carriage, on three-feet ice, more than once in last April. The
cold is more intense, yet more uniform than with us. The
average cold from the 1st of November to the 1st of March
is equal to the coldest week in our winter, while many
weeks there are twice as cold, ranging from fifteen to
twenty-five degrees of Reaumur, which is two and one-
fourth of Fahrenheit. The nights are long, from 4 o'clock
in the evening to 8 in the morning. The sled is in
constant use in the winter, and is a cheerful exercise, when
one is wrapt in furs. The rooms are admirably heated, so
that in the coldest weather I slept on a mattress under one
comforter. This mode of imparting a uniform temperature
to their rooms is worthy of introduction into our own
country, especially the northern part of it. The chimney
is, indeed, an ornamental piece of furniture; it is made of
brick, covered with porcelain, has flues, and, when the
wood has burned to a coal, the mouth below and the flues
above are closed up, which causes the heat from the bricks
to spread gradually over the room. Unless the cold is very
severe, one fire is sufficient for the twenty-four hours; and,
by means of a private passage, the servant heats the room
without the necessity of coming in with the wood — a fact
which will be appreciated by all neat housekeepers, and by
those who do not choose their slumbers in the morning to
be disturbed in the preparations for rendering their bed-
rooms comfortable, both of which classes of persons I have
doubtless now the honor of addressing. Sleds and ice
hills, so peculiar in Russia, are the amusements of the day;
while the long nights are occupied with soirées, balls, operas,
and theatres, and even these engage for a portion of the night
the attention of the *literati* and officers of state. I enjoyed the
exhilarating exercise of being drawn in a Laplander's sled,

with four reindeer, on the ice of the Neva; and I often
witnessed the small boats, shod with iron like the sleds,
drawn by the wind in an incredible period of time from
St. Petersburg to Cronstadt, the great naval port. The summer of Russia is as remarkable as the winter; the influence
of the spring being scarcely felt. Not a bud is seen before
the 1st of May, and the full-blown leaf is found on the 1st of
June. The growth of vegetables is remarkably rapid, rendering them tender. The nights are the reverse of those in
winter. You may read at midnight; and the people walk
the streets until 11; at 1, dawn commences, and the sun
is up at 2, having set the previous evening at 9. For six
weeks, in midsummer, the heat is oppressive in the sun,
from 11 to 3; but you sleep under a coverlid, and thus
find the invigorating effects of which you are denied in the
region of the tropics.

"The Nobility of Russia consists of some ten or twelve
grades ; the highest in rank are the descendants of the
ancient princes, of the dukedom prior to the Empire, and
those who are created by the Emperor in consideration of
eminent public services ; then counts; then an inferior grade
of princes. All officers of the army who reach the grade
of colonel are considered as ennobled; but society, as the
higher circles are called, consists only of the first four or
five grades. These all receive a liberal education, and many
of them are permitted to travel into other countries, and
are distinguished by their polished manners and their intellectual accomplishments. Many of the nobility have immense estates, including often ten thousand serfs, with more
land than they can cultivate. The deference paid to them
by the peasantry is more marked than with our republican
notions we could conceive it to be possible. It will be difficult, in the limit allowed to these remarks, to dwell upon
the manners and customs of the nobility or of the etiquette
which is so exacting at the Court; but I may be allowed to
pause a moment on the female character of the wealthier
classes. These are educated in a liberal style, and many of
14

their accomplishments are useful as well as ornamental. They have a fine taste for music and embroidery, of which latter I have some elegant specimens — a souvenir — in return for American books. The children of both sexes are taught, from an early period, to observe the most courteous manner, and a laudable neatness of dress, in which they as much deserve to be models to our own children as in their remarkable efficiency in the knowledge of modern languages. I have often heard the children at the family table speak in four languages: French, German, Russian, and English, and acquired in the order mentioned. The three qualities for which the ladies merit particular notice consists in their graceful movements, neat costumes, combining richness with simplicity, and unaffected manners; in all these they excel the most intellectual English, and the sprightly though less dignified French, and, I hope I may be pardoned for saying that, in these respects, they are in advance of our own ladies; though in freshness of beauty, in symmetry of form, intellectual vivacity, and real nobility of character, every American, who travels abroad, will admit that our own have no superiors in any land.

"The second class of persons, in Russia, consisting of the various grades of merchants, the shopkeepers, and handicraft tradesmen, have many peculiar qualities; they adhere, in dress, to the national costume, though in a style more European than that of the serf. As traders, they are astute and enterprising; and Peter well described them when he told the Jews, on entering his Empire, that they were welcome to cheat his subjects if they could. This class is making rapid strides in intelligence and in the useful qualities of the citizens, and form, with the serfs, objects of deep solicitude in the ameliorating measures of the Emperor. The serfs, amounting to forty millions, of which fifteen millions belong to the Crown, are objects of great interest to the traveller. Up to the middle of the sixteenth century there were no slaves in Russia, except a few prisoners of war; and the peasants, or agricultural work-

men, the most numerous class of inhabitants in Russia,
could change their abode once a year, on the 23d of April,
St. George's day.   One of the Czars, or rulers, Boris Goda-
noff, about the middle of the sixteenth century, decreed that,
in future, no peasant should have the right of changing his
master, and should remain forever the resident of the same
place, so that by selling the landed property the peasants
also were sold.   The successors of the Czar Boris, up to the
time of the Emperor Alexander (1800), gave away a large
quantity of Crown land to the nobility, as a remuneration
for their services, and transferred the peasants who resided
on those lands; thus converting free peasants into serfs, or
slaves,' up to the eighteenth century, when Catharine II.
declared that they were not slaves, but only vassals or
peasants attached to the glebe.   The Emperor Alexander,
at his accession to the throne, prohibited the further distri-
bution of Government lands inhabited by peasants, and in
1815 undertook the task of liberating the peasants of Russia.
He persuaded a majority of the proprietors of estates in the
three western provinces of the Empire, called the Baltic
provinces, containing two millions of inhabitants, to give
liberty to their serfs on certain conditions.   These were
discussed by a committee of the proprietors, and approved
by the Emperor.   No disturbance grew out of the arrangement, and in 1823 there remained no slaves in these provinces.   If I had the time, I could describe the process of
this gradual emancipation; merely remarking that the lib-
erated serfs were not allowed to leave those provinces, nor
to go into the interior provinces where slavery still exists.
In the last twenty years the Emperor Nicholas has enacted
several laws securing privileges to the serfs in the remaining provinces of Russia, such as that no serf could be sold
separately from his family, nor the family from the estate,
nor that the proprietor should require of the serf more than
three days labor in the week.   Half of the whole number
of serfs do not work on the land of their proprietors, but
pay him a certain sum, and receive from him a portion of

land.   Many peasants buy their own time, and are engaged as artisans or shopkeepers in the various towns.

"The first impression of admiration that strikes the traveller, on entering St. Petersburg, is directed to the deep, clear river, noble quarries of granite with iron railings, splendid streets, magnificent palaces, and the hundred churches with lofty spires and gilded domes; and he then turns with astonishment from these monuments of civilization, to look at the people who have reared them — serfs, with their long beards, clad in sheep-skin coats with the wool inside. The resources of Russia are of vast extent; independently of the productions of her soil and of her workshops, &c., she has great mineral wealth; gold, platina, copper, and iron abound in greater quantities than in any other portion of Europe, if not of the globe, though no mines of coal are to be found.   The consumption of this article, at St. Petersburg, is supplied as ballast in the ships, and is as cheap as at New Castle.   In her geographical position so compact; in her military capacities, in her warlike character, and her vast energies, concentrated by the genius of one mind, Russia may be regarded as the first Northern power in Europe, if not the equal of any on the Continent. Like our own beloved land, she is the child of the eighteenth century.   In the last one hundred years she has advanced as rapidly as her neighbors in all that constitutes the strength of a State, if we except the results which flow only from the diffusion of intelligence among the masses. Like our own country, she is formidable in her offensive, as well as defensive, attitude: she by her isolated position and gigantic army; we by our extended coast and efficient marine.   Under a proper system of culture, she, like the United States, possesses ample means for feeding her own people, and of contributing to the wants of other nations, — in all substantial respects, the two powers are the most independent on the globe.   They have no conflicting points of contact; they are destined to be the best neighbors, because they are so far off.   The power of steam is working wonders in both; railroads will give them permanent tranquillity, for in the concentrated means of war are found the surest guarantees of peace. The capacity which their internal facilities afford for precipitating a large military force from the interior to the frontier will preserve both from invasion; while, in Russia, the vast railroad contemplated by the Emperor, for uniting the Baltic with the Black Sea and the Caspian, will give him the power to invade the contiguous nations at the same time his standing army, permitted from this power of sudden concentration to be reduced in numbers and expense, is engaged in preserving the public peace at home. With this interesting nation we have always maintained a friendly intercourse. It is a sublime spectacle, worthy the contemplation of other Powers, to see two great nations, the most extensive in territory and resources, in the Old and in the New World, always living in peace. As to them, the Temple of Janus has been always shut; may it never be opened! And may I not renew to you an expression of the sentiment in which, with the independence and courtesy of a Kentuckian, I indulged in my last interview with the Emperor, that the day might soon arrive when the power of the United States and Russia, by sea and by land, should be such as to command all the nations of the earth to be at peace.

" I have only a moment to allude to the Government and Administration, and seize the occasion to introduce reflections of a sagacious and accomplished American, recently at St. Petersburg. 'The will of the Emperor embraces the executive, legislative, and judicial power. He is the supreme judge, the commander of the armies, the head of the Church. The Senate consists of many worthy men, distinguished by their learning, or the services they have rendered the State. They are appointed by his Majesty, and by his consent or command they ratify treaties, receive petitions, etc.; they have no authority, except as wise and prudent counsellors. The internal and external interests of the Empire are regulated and superintended by various

departments, over which the Emperor appoints a Minister.
The Russian Territory is divided into many governments,
superintending the ecclesiastical matters, education, ways,
and communications, civil or secret, and military police,
etc., dependent on the chief department at St. Petersburg.
The police master of a village, town, or district, is the
judge and jury in almost all kinds of proceedings; he is a
very powerful individual, and much respected. Imagine,
if you can, our President, the supreme ruler of the six-and-
twenty States of the Union, the governors of the States
acting as his deputies, waiting for his commands, and you
have almost a daguerreotype illustration of the whole gov-
ernmental apparatus of the Czar. With the imperfection
of such a machine, the wonder is how it is kept in motion,
and how it effects so much. The merchants — the great
merchants of the large commercial cities — have a resort,
in civil cases, by permission of the government, to ref-
erees; and an appeal may be had thence to the 'minister of
the department of commerce, that is, in truth, to the Emperor.'

"It would appear then, from this graphic description,
that the Emperor is the beginning and the ending of
all things in his dominions. And what shall I say of
this remarkable personage, who unites in his appearance
and character the dignity and intellectual developments
of our first Governor, and the symmetry and personal
beauty of Benjamin Howard? and what more could I say
of him, than that he would have been selected, from his
commanding presence and address, to be the leader of the
choicest sons of Kentucky who have ever gone forth from
her bosom to advance the national renown! He only
needs to have mingled in the eventful scenes encountered
by Louis Philippe, and to have suffered a similar adversity,
to place him at the head of the sovereigns of Europe in the
great qualities of intellectual energy, accomplished address,
and sagacious statesmanship. It should not be a matter of
wonder, that a self-willed monarch, with absolute power,

should be sometimes capricious, and even tyrannical ; the
infirmities of human nature would render this probable, and
the momentous interests, domestic and foreign, of a great
Empire claiming his attention, would doubtless suffer many
acts of injustice, oppression, and cruelty, to be perpetrated
by his subordinates of which he would be ignorant.   It is
sufficient for other nations to know, that he is laboring to
carry out the plans of Peter, and that he has succeeded in
advancing his peasantry to a higher civilization than that
attained by the same class in England under Henry the
Eighth.   In the broad Catholic sense of patriotism, he stands
out the great man of his country, devoting his energies to
the preservation of the nationality of his people ; and whatever we may think of a government which is the antipode
of our own, it is not to be denied that his death, in the
present condition of Russia, would be a great national calamity.   But we are not permitted to estimate the patriotism
of the rulers of other countries by our own standard.   In
the Indian sense of the term, Tecumseh was a patriot ; he
devoted his great energies to the preservation of the distinctive character, and what he deemed to be the rights of
the Northwestern tribes.   During an interview with General
Harrison, previous to the war, he referred, with great eloquence, to the plan which the United States had adopted
of purchasing lands from the individual tribes, and which
he regarded as a mighty river about to overflow his people,
avowing that his own plan of a confederacy of the tribes not
to suffer individual tribes to sell, was the dam he was erecting to arrest the progress of the flood.   Addressing the
General, he said : ' If your Great Father, who sits beyond
the mountains and drinks his wine, shall persevere in this
system, you and I will have to fight it out.'   And nobly did
he redeem his pledge : at the memorable victory of the
Thames he sealed with his blood his devotion to his nations, and, whenever the history of this continent shall be
fully written, Tecumseh will be described as possessing the
management of Philip, the military genius of Pontiac, and

the valor and eloquence of Buchonghelass, who, upon the occasion of holding a treaty with General George Rogers Clarke, the Hannibal of the West, and two other commissioners, entered the Council House, and paying no attention to the latter, advanced to General Clarke and thanked the Great Spirit that he had that day brought together two such great warriors as Buchonghelass and General Clarke.

"One word as to the character of the Secret Police, whose sagacity will compare with the days of Napoleon. Two anecdotes, occurring during my residence, may suffice. An American merchant, son of a venerable merchant of Philadelphia, came to St. Petersburg, and on presenting himself, according to the custom, at the office of the Minister of Police, was informed that fourteen years ago he had visited St. Petersburg, and that his objects were so and so. Says the Minister, ' Will you have the kindness to state what are your objects in the present visit ? ' Upon another occasion, a Frenchman presented himself at the office. The Minister instantly handed him a passport to the frontier. The Frenchman was astonished, and asked why he could not be permitted to remain. The Minister said : ' You were born in such a village in France ; you have lived in such and such places ; and you have killed eight men in duels. We want no such person here : take this passport, and allow me to recommend you never to attempt again to enter Russia.' What a noble example does this policy present for the imitation of other nations ! "

An effort was made in the Whig State Convention of 1848 to secure to Colonel Todd the nomination for governor of Kentucky. He was not mixed up with the cliques in that party, known as Letcher and Owsley cliques. He was a favorite with the most prominent men of both wings of the party.

But Mr. Graves, of the Owsley clique, and Dixon

of the Letcher clique, had long been aspirants for the position. They had energy and ambition. They carried a large majority of the counties in primary assemblies. And although either would have preferred Colonel Todd to his rival, there was such a spirit between them that it appeared that they would contend for the ascendancy in the Convention.

Colonel Todd supposed that he would be defeated on the second ballot. In this state of affairs, he addressed a note to the Convention, withdrawing his name from the contest in order to secure unanimity in the ranks of the party. This movement led to the immediate nomination of Mr. Crittenden, which induced the other candidates to retire from the contest. Quite a number of distinguished politicians afterwards expressed the opinion that Colonel Todd would have received a much stronger support than that given to Mr. Crittenden.

In 1850 Colonel Todd, in company with General Robert B. Campbell and Oliver P. Temple, accepted a mission tendered them by the United States Government, to treat with the Indian tribes on the border of the United States and Mexico. I find in the *National Intelligencer*, of October, 1850, the following reference to these gentlemen and their mission:

"Distinguished as have been the services of these gentlemen in other higher, but scarcely more responsible trusts, the country has an assurance that an important duty of the Administration has been ably discharged, especially in providing for the fulfilment of one of the difficult stipulations of the treaty of peace with Mexico. By an act of the last session of Congress, the President was required to appoint a commission to obtain statistical information of, and to

15

form treaties with, the various tribes of Indians on the border of the United States and Mexico. The importance of this trust has not for many years been exceeded, and is without precedent but in the plenary power given by Mr. Jefferson to Governor William H. Harrison, to treat with all the tribes of the Northwest. In parting with these gentlemen on this distant and perilous service, we cannot but express the interest which we, in common with all their friends, feel for their success."

After the mission terminated, Colonel Todd drew up the report, from which we make the subjoined extracts. The report is not only remarkable for the service performed by these gentlemen, but for the thorough knowledge they displayed in regard to the Indian character. The long experience Colonel Todd had in Indian affairs peculiarly fitted him for the duties of the Commission. After describing the causes of delay at New Orleans, which was aggravated by the non-arrival of arms they were led to believe would meet them on their arrival in that city, the report says:

"General Campbell remained in New Orleans until December 8th, waiting the necessary orders from the War Department; the other Commissioners proceeding on the 1st of December to Galveston, thence to Austin, the seat of government of Texas, with a view to a consultation with Governor Bell, as suggested in a conversation held by the Commissioners with Senator Rusk, of New Orleans.

"We beg leave to refer to our despatch of December 21st from San Antonio as furnishing an account of the interview with Senator Rusk and Governor Bell, and of our intention to proceed to El Paso and collect the Apaches, and of our recommendation as to our future Indian policy in Texas. In that despatch we invited the attention of the Department to the necessity and importance of an increased appropriation for our Commission, and a separate escort of cavalry with which to penetrate into the interior of the country, instead of depending upon the escort accompanying the boundary party.

" We regretted that we could not reach San Antonio and make the necessary preparations to accompany the boundary party from that point to El Paso on the Rio Grande. That Commission had left San Antonio early in November, and a reference to the date of our instructions received at Washington, and the distance of three thousand miles to San Antonio, apart from the delay in that city to equip the Commission for a wilderness journey of six hundred and fifty miles, will show the utter improbability that we could have arrived in time to proceed with that party ; nor, indeed, was it vitally important that we should reach El Paso until Spring, from the almost certainty that the boundary party would not enter the Rocky Mountains until the milder season should appear, — a conjecture which subsequent events have reduced to a certainty, inasmuch as it is not known that the party had yet penetrated the mountains.

" It may be proper to state that the position of Secretary to the Commission, the only office under our appointment whose pay is fixed in our instructions, was conferred, December 4th, on Major Robert H. Armstrong, of Tennessee. Immediately upon our arrival at San Antonio, Major Babbit, U. S. Quartermaster at that point, called to inform us that he had received instructions to furnish transportation for our party to El Paso. As he did not favor us with an opportunity to examine his instructions, and having no reason to suppose there was any doubt as to their real import, we contented ourselves with awaiting his arrangements on the subject, which he stated would be completed by the 8th of January ; and we did not learn until the 6th of January, a few days prior to the time fixed for our departure, that, from a more critical examination of his instructions, he found his authority to provide transportation was confined exclusively to the escort accompanying us. In this exigency, and from a statement which he submitted to us as to the enormous expense attending our journey in mid-winter as compared with that in a period of grass, we determined to suspend our movements, go into camp, and await instructions from the Department. The letter of Quartermaster Babbit will present a full view of this subject, and we request that it may be regarded as a part of this report.

"The decision to remain at San Antonio until the season of grass realized a saving of many thousands to the public treasury. Subsequent events have confirmed the wisdom of that determination. The refusal of Congress to increase our appropriation, as well as the reorganization of the Indian Bureau, by which our powers to make Indian treaties were abrogated, would have placed us in a situation truly embarrassing, if we had gone in mid-winter to El Paso, and thus have exhausted the existing appropriation.

"It is competent for Congress to abandon a system at one session which it instituted at a previous session, but the prudence of our delay at San Antonio is not the less apparent from this vacillation in the public council. During our necessary detention at San Antonio, it was our wish to seize every opportunity of procuring any information that might be useful to our future operations. With this view, Colonel Temple was deputed, early in February, from the camp beyond San Antonio to proceed to Fort Martin Scott, the military post (the most remote to the Northwest), to be present at the time specified in the treaty with Judge Rollins, where the Indians were to be reassembled. An unfortunate discrepancy between the parties as to the precise day for the Council prevented Colonel Temple from meeting the Indians as he had anticipated ; they having appeared the week before, and then returned to their distant camps.

"We deemed it important during the delay in making preparations for the journey to El Paso to open a communication with the Governor of Texas in reference to the probable prospect of that State consenting to the establishment of a separate boundary for the Indians in her limits; and, with that view, addressed a letter, of the 2d of January, to Governor Bell, to which, and to our despatch of the 4th of January, enclosing it to the Department, we ask to refer as a part of the report. The views we have felt it our duty to submit to the Department, on this interesting subject, are further illustrated in our despatch of the 13th of February, and that of the 15th of March, enclosing a memorandum of an interview with Governor Bell, — all of which may be regarded as entering into this report.

"We beg leave also to refer to the despatch of the 4th of April, with a memorandum, touching the interview of one of the Commissioners of Eagle Pass with Coacohee, or 'Wild Cat,' the celebrated Seminole chief, now residing in Mexico."

The report also makes mention of Colonel Todd being deputed by his colleagues to go to Washington for the further views of the Government, while the other Commissioners remained in Texas until his return. They all, then, repaired to Washington for the purpose of surrendering their commissions. The report concludes with the following :

"In the expenditure which we thought the public interest demanded, we have included five hundred pounds of the new improved meat called the Beef Biscuit, manufactured at Galveston, Texas. We suppose, this amount was necessary for an expedition originally contemplated to continue two years. This discovery we regard as a national benefit, and we recommend its use in all military and exploring expeditions. In relation to the Indian agencies in Texas, on which our instructions require us to report, we have no hesitation in suggesting to the Department the policy of recommending to Congress the creation of a superintendent of Indian Affairs in Texas, in connection with sub-agencies in the present

plan of several independent agencies. The simple statement of this policy carries with it the obvious advantages
of uniform and harmonious action, and is sustained by the
previous practice of the Government in conducting its
Indian relations in other sections of our country. The
objection (which it is hoped may soon be removed) that
the United States have no authority to regulate Indian
affairs in Texas, applies as well to the present system of
Indian agencies as to that we have suggested; and there
are considerations connected with Indian affairs in that
State which peculiarly recommend this policy with the
frontier from whence the public peace of the settled district
of Texas and Mexico is constantly exposed to interrup-
tions and the inhabitants to pillage and murder from roving
Indians to whom no separate territory has been assigned,
and over whom, consequently, the intercourse-laws of the
United States have not been extended.

" In venturing, therefore, to recommend the establishment
of a superintendent of Indian affairs, we pre-suppose that it
is the purpose, at an early day, of the United States, as well
as of Texas, to enter into suitable arrangements by which
the Indians shall be induced to remain in a specified boundary, and their tranquillity so secured as to offer no possible
pretext for the wars in which they would be exterminated.
This salutary, philanthropic policy may tend to their civilization by teaching them to cultivate the soil, and acquire
individual property, and domesticate themselves, so far at
least as to become herdsmen instead of living like wander-
ing Arabs. It is not necessary, in this view of the subject,
to anticipate the condition of things, when the wave of
colonized population shall approach the specified boundary,
urging their removal to a more distant frontier. Their
ultimate fate may be safely confided to the wisdom and
magnanimity of those who may be called in the next
generation to preside over the national councils.

" The present path of duty and honor is plain. Both
humanity and economy concur in advocating the system

we have suggested as proper for the guidance of our future Indian relations on the borders of the United States and Mexico. This system contemplates arrangements by which incursions into Mexico, as well as Texas, shall be restrained, and the separate territory proposed to be secured in Texas lies north of the route usually travelled to El Paso and New Mexico. A boundary having this beneficial provision on the entire route to the Pacific, will therefore offer inducements to a cordon of settlements along the borders of the United States and Mexico, which, with the military advantages of a railroad, will supersede the necessity of any considerable expenditure in the establishment of military posts.

" In this view of the subject, we regard a railroad, so far as its establishment may be within the provision of the Constitution, contiguous to the route now in process of demarkation, and extending to the Pacific, as possessing eminent tendencies to fulfil our treaty stipulations, one of the important objects contemplated by our instructions. Without any designs to disparage other routes to the Pacific, we may be permitted to speak of the great advantages which the climate and topography on this route present, for the Gila, erroneously estimated at sixteen hundred miles, is believed to be, in the opinion of competent officers of the Topographical Bureau, not more than twelve hundred; and along this route the depressions in the Rocky Mountains are pre-eminently advantageous for the construction of a railroad, while all the approaches through Texas to El Paso on the Rio Grande present the most inviting considerations for the great object.

" It is needless to expatiate upon the value of a railroad communication across the continent *within our own borders*, whether we look at it in a commercial, political, or military point of view. As a bond of union between the States on the Atlantic and Pacific, its importance cannot be exaggerated ; and, in the event of war with a maritime power, the facility which it would afford for the rapid transportation and sudden concentration of an armed force, will render our possessions on the Pacific as impregnable, as the late war with Great Britain proved our invincibility along the Atlantic, Mississippi, and Lake coasts.

" In closing this report, and terminating our commission, we have the honor to state that we have deposited with the proper authorities money and property somewhat less than fourteen thousand dollars of the thirty thousand dollars appropriated by the Act of Congress of the 30th of September, 1850."

This is probably the only instance in the history of the Government, when any moneys, appropriated in this way, have ever been returned to the Treasury. It was indeed discreditable to Congress that further efforts were not made to secure the invaluable services of the accomplished gentlemen.

The report is particularly interesting, inasmuch as it refers to the construction of a railroad to the Pacific.

Colonel Todd was among the first of American statesmen who advocated and demonstrated the practicability of such a road. The difficulties to be overcome, at that time, were indeed great ; they were almost insurmountable. The enemies of the road did all they could against it, and proclaimed those who were in favor of it to be wild and thoughtless schemers. It was said that Sierra Nevada was impassable ; that snow and ice were piled from forty to sixty feet high ; that there was scarcely room for a driver to walk by the side of his mule ; that travellers were often lost and frozen to death in the mountains, &c. Colonel Todd was constantly busy with his pen agitating the subject.

In the Report of the United States Board of Engineers sent out by the War Department, the plan he suggested was the most highly commended. Almost everything he wrote received the attention of the leading journalists, the statesmen, and capitalists, of the country. The friends of the route through Texas to El Paso on the Rio Grande, and the friends of the Central route, united their strength in Congress, and gave a two-thirds vote in favor of it. The measure would have certainly passed, had not Texas resolved to secede. The bill loaned the credit of the Government to the Central route to the extent of ninety million dollars, and sixty million dollars to the Southern route. These loans were to be returned to the Government in transportation.

The war broke out, and raged with uninterrupted fury. Millions upon millions had been spent to put down the rebellion; but nothing, it would seem, could destroy the interest taken in the Pacific railroad even then.

Colonel Todd's observation, in the report quoted above, that the construction of the road would induce a cordon of settlements along the borders of the frontier States, thereby doing away with the necessity of military outposts, was at that time an argument in favor of the road.

The average cost of a regiment of soldiers is said to be more than a million a year; and, when we consider the number of troops required to quell the disposition to war on the part of the North American Indians, we can see at a glance the force of the argument.

16

CHAPTER IX.

Colonel Todd prepares a Series of Articles on Texas — Letter from Daniel Webster to Colonel Todd — Colonel Todd prepares a Sketch of Tecumseh for the *Louisville Journal* — He proposes to write the Early History of Kentucky — An Incident in the College Life of Colonel Todd — His Confidential Report to the War Department in 1815.

D URING Colonel Todd's sojourn in Texas as a Commissioner, he prepared for the press a series of articles on the agricultural and mineral resources of Texas. Their publication attracted no little attention in the South and Southwest. The intimate acquaintance he displayed with geological and other scientific subjects well merited the commendation he received.

Colonel Todd is the author of the best account of the battle of the Thames ever published.

The following beautiful letter from Daniel Webster to Colonel Todd shows the esteem in which that great statesman and orator held the subject of this memoir, and the great confidence he had in his judgment and integrity:

"WASHINGTON, November 6th, 1851.

"MY DEAR SIR: I am very much obliged to you for your friendly feelings and the very favorable sentiments towards me, which you are pleased to express. We were intimately acquainted formerly, in the days of the good President Harrison, who was, I know, your fast and unalterable friend. I shall always cherish the highest respect for his memory and character.

"I should be very glad to see you. Nobody can tell,

my dear sir, what times are before us. I think that good men, and lovers of their country, should stand together, and act together. I have the truest confidence in you, both as to your fidelity and ability. You are in the vigor of life, active, and well known to very many good men and true friends of the Government; and, certainly, you can do much good. You need not doubt of my good wishes now, and at all times. I repeat that, if not inconvenient, I hope you will come this way.

" Yours truly,   DANIEL WEBSTER."
" To COLONEL C. S. TODD."

In 1862 Colonel Todd wrote a very charming sketch, for the *Louisville Journal*, of Tecumseh, the great Indian warrior. This article completely settles the vexed question as to "who killed Tecumseh." The manner in which Colonel Todd disposes of the claims of the many aspirants to the honor of having killed Tecumseh is so clear and pointed, and at the same time so severe and just, that no one, I think, who has read the article, would care to open the subject for discussion again.

The account given by the English historian, James, is completely overthrown in Colonel Todd's article. James ascribed the honor of killing the gifted King of the Woods to Colonel Richard M. Johnson, of Kentucky. We learn from Colonel Todd's article that General Harrison was the only officer in the army, engaged in the battle, who had ever seen Tecumseh; and that Harrison did not know that Tecumseh was killed until some time after the engagement. Colonel Todd also says that all accounts of Harrison's recognizing the body of Tecumseh, and expressing the opinion that he fell by the hand of Colonel Johnson, are fabled and entitled to no credit whatever. It is not known who killed him. That this subject should attract so much attention is not at all strange, for Tecumseh was one of the most remarkable men that ever lived. He displayed not only the greatest qualities of a warrior, but of an orator and a statesman. He seemed ever to be actuated by the loftiest ambition. Though his hatred for the whites was severe and unmeasured, his mode of warfare was wholly free from the brutal cruelty of his race, while his ideas of honor were chivalric in every sense of the word. Had he lived, it is not improbable that much would have been done toward carrying out the great object of his life, viz.: that of collecting together the scattered tribes of North America, and establishing an Indian monarchy on the continent.

Colonel Todd, a short time before his death, was at work upon a series of articles in reference to the Early History of Kentucky. It is to be regretted that he did not live to complete them.

George D. Prentice, of the *Louisville Journal*, said, when he heard that Colonel Todd was engaged on the History of Kentucky : " There is no man in all the world so well qualified for the task as he. I shall await the perusal of Colonel Todd's work with no ordinary pleasure."

An incident happened to Colonel Todd while at college, which I will relate. The Hon. John J. Barbour, of Virginia, nephew of Governor Barbour of that State, very grossly insulted Colonel Todd. Barbour was armed at the time; but in almost the same instant that he gave the insult, Colonel Todd turned upon him and thrashed him severely with his walking-cane. Soon after this castigation, Barbour sent a challenge to Colonel Todd, who could not accept it, as Bishop Madison was his security in a civil process to keep the peace. Colonel Todd, in declining the challenge, explained his reason for so doing; but stated he would fight him as soon as he was released from his bond to keep the peace. Barbour was afterward a member of Congress from Virginia, and nominated General Pierce for the Presidency at the Baltimore Convention.

When Colonel Todd returned from his mission to South America, Barbour endeavored to reinstate himself in his favor, and wrote a letter to him, in 1824, to that effect. I have the original letter, together with a copy of Colonel Todd's reply to it, and I see no good reason for not publishing them. The following is the correspondence :

" WASHINGTON, April 15th, 1824.

"SIR : — Juvenile attachments are said to be the most lasting which the human heart can cherish. It is equally true that juvenile feuds are the most fleeting and transitory. What our experience has been in regard to this influence should not, I think, at this moment be a matter of inquiry. For myself, I say to you candidly and fearlessly that I desire to revive the former of these sentiments, and give the latter to oblivion. I shall not do you the injustice to suspect that this note may be misconstrued. On the contrary, I shall be gratified to learn a reciprocal inclination in your breast.

"I am, Sir, respectfully yours,   J. J. BARBOUR."

" BROWN'S HOTEL, April 16th, 1824.

"SIR — I have been favored by the receipt of your note of yesterday, and hasten to assure you of my concurrence in the sentiments you have suggested. The unpleasant controversy to which you refer was very shortly afterward consigned to oblivion. I am not aware that I had then, or

at any subsequent period, cause to revive a recollection of it
It is unnecessary for me to say, that it will give me pleasure
to unite with you in reviving and promoting a friendly feeling and intercourse, and with that view I shall be happy to
see you whenever your convenience may permit.

"I am, Sir, very respectfully yours,

"C. S. Todd."

Circumstances, however, prevented them from renewing their acquaintance. Barbour called to see
Todd, but did not find him at home; and when Todd
returned the visit, Barbour was absent.

I must not forget to make mention of the Confidential report Colonel Todd made to the War
Department in 1815.

The report was forwarded to the board of officers
selected by the President to arrange the peace, and
to reduce the nominal amount of the army of fifty
thousand to ten thousand men. By this arrangement
four-fifths of the officers were to be removed.

Colonel Todd's report elicited the highest commendation for its discriminating fairness and impartiality. General Winfield Scott was President of
the Board, and remarked to a party of friends at the
house of General Preston, that, as General Harrison
had resigned, and Generals Jackson and Gaines were
absent, the Board looked to Colonel Todd's report for
information in regard to the officers in the West, and
that the Board regarded the report as the most intelligent and practical of any rendered to the Department, and that they made it the basis of their selection.

Colonel Todd was then only twenty-four years of
age. It is worthy of note that the new Register contained no name on which he had placed a black mark.

CHAPTER X.

Colonel Todd takes an Active Part in the Taylor Campaign — His Characteristics as a Popular Orator — His Opinions of Jefferson and Jackson — His Acquaintance with the Presidents — His Admiration of Madison — His Accomplishments as a Man of the World — His Moral Characteristics — Anecdote of Bernadotte, King of Sweden.

IN 1848 Colonel Todd took an active part in the Presidential contest between General Taylor and General Cass. Colonel Todd spoke at nearly all the large political meetings in Ohio. He also addressed the people at various points in Pennsylvania, New York, Massachusetts, and Connecticut. His finest speech was at Lowell, Mass. I have never read an abler and a more conscientious and painstaking document than his speech at Lowell. It is a thorough and a complete elucidation of the political questions of the day, as well as a just and noble tribute to the distinguished services of General Taylor. It was not without its effects in that canvass. General Taylor was very proud of it, and said that he did not fear the result of the contest when such able speeches were made in his behalf. Colonel Todd's arguments were always closely considered, and in every way calculated to assert truth and to refute falsehood. There was no clap-trap nonsense about him; nothing said merely for effect, and his opponents were usually so hemmed in by the array of facts he brought against them, that there was not the slightest gap left open for escape. He was thoroughly versed in the history of the country, and was never at a loss

in regard to facts and dates of important political
events. I remember asking him, on one occasion,
what he thought of the Jeffersonian Democracy, and
he said: "I suppose, in speaking of the Jeffersonian
Democracy, you make a distinction between it and
the Jackson Democracy?" I was about to say that
the difference was not very plainly marked, when he
said: "General Jackson and Mr. Van Buren introduced a new Democratic party, after the old parties,
the Federal and Democratic, had passed away during
the administration of Mr. Monroe. From 1798 to
1815 a great struggle existed between the old parties, and it is a singular fact that General Jackson
recommended to Mr. Monroe to discard politics altogether in the selection of his Cabinet, and urged him
to select from both parties. Such was Jackson's own
practice when he came into power; for instance, he
appointed Livingston and McLean, who were strong
Federalists, and formed a new party of those who
had voted for him, and called it the Democratic
party.

"Jackson and Jefferson," Colonel Todd said, "were
indeed great leaders, but with altogether different
principles and temperaments. Jackson had great
genius and a thorough knowledge of men and things,
united to an indomitable will, which enabled him, with
scarcely the ordinary accomplishments of a gentleman, to guide the policy of the nation. Jefferson could
not do more, though he was splendidly educated, and
had mingled with the greatest scholars and intellects
of Europe and America. He had talent for control-
ling public affairs. He was a strong man, as well as
a learned man. He was both a statesman and a
philosopher."

I then asked Colonel Todd what he thought of Randall's Life of Jefferson. Colonel Todd said: "It is a fine account of Jefferson; but that author, in publishing Jefferson's writings, published too much, for Jefferson was of the French school in both religion and politics. He loved his country, I believe, with unabated ardor, and appears to a splendid advantage in many phases of character; but he will not go down to posterity with the pure and unsullied principles of Madison, who was at once the ablest and the most beautiful of all our public men."

Colonel Todd once told me that he had seen all the American Presidents, with the exception of Washington and the elder Adams, and had an intimate personal acquaintance with most of them. He said: "I saw Mr. Jefferson on the day he left his office; I being present at the inauguration of Madison, having gone to Washington for the purpose of seeing my father, who was then one of the Judges of the Supreme Court. My intercourse was very intimate with Madison, and Monroe, and John Quincy Adams, and Harrison, and, more or less so, with Tyler, Taylor, Fillmore, Pierce, Buchanan, and Lincoln."

At another time he said: "I have many letters from prominent men throughout the country, and there is not one among them that is not worthy of your attention and perusal. I treasure most the letters of Harrison, Mr. Clay, General Cass, and Mr. Webster. I have a number of Buchanan's letters; but I never like to read them. He was an old Federalist, turning to a Jackson Democrat."

On another occasion, in speaking to me of our Presidents, Colonel Todd said: "It is a creditable

17

fact that every one of our Presidents selected one of the ablest men in his party for Secretary of State; and this fact has rendered our correspondence with foreign countries fully as good as the most distinguished State papers of Great Britain and France, if not better."

I asked him what he thought of the correspondence he had with some of the distinguished Russian statesmen, and he said: "The State papers are generally indifferent; those of Count Nesselrode are the only ones that will at all compare favorably with ours."

In regard to Jefferson's State papers, he said: "Among the papers of George Wythe, of Virginia, who was one of the committee to report on the Declaration of Independence, was the original report of Mr. Jefferson, which Judge Wythe says was 'altered for the worse' by the committee. It was arranged, as you doubtless know, that each member should prepare a paper to be submitted to a sub-committee, or two, for consideration and report. Mr. Jefferson, being the first-named upon the committee, was called upon first, and, after his paper was read, the other gentlemen declined to read theirs, and the sub-committee accepted Mr. Jefferson's. This was, of course, Jefferson's ablest State paper, if not the greatest paper ever written. His Inaugural Address is also a masterpiece of composition."

In person, Colonel Todd was rather above than below the medium height, and was stoutly and compactly built. His complexion was fair, and his eyes were of a dark hazel, and of a singular brilliancy of expression. His bearing and manners were dignified and elegant in the extreme. He was a thorough gentleman of the old school. No prince or courtier ever transcended him in politeness. He had one of the clearest and richest and most musical voices I ever heard. ,He was altogether the best conversationist with whom I have ever been thrown in contact. He was a model of a drawing-room companion. He knew how to show, to both gentlemen and ladies, those little attentions which come only from gentle blood and good breeding. He dearly loved children; he would take them for hours at a time on his knee, and listen to their prattle with as much attention apparently as he would listen to the wisdom of a philosopher; he had always a welcoming smile to the little ones who entered his room, and, when engaged in writing, he would cheerfully lay aside his work and join in a romp, or play, with them. He believed that the only happiness in the world consisted in doing good, and he did good for others all the days of his life. He was ever ready to forget and forgive those who had wronged him; he could not be otherwise than just and true and noble, for he was himself a living and an essential truth. Heaven was kindly to him to the last, and ever kept his heart full of pure and sweet and gentle emotions. It was a common saying among his friends that he never grew old; and, indeed, I have never known any one who seemed to preserve to such an advanced age the vigor and freshness of young manhood. When nearly eighty years of age, he did not look to me more than fifty; and when fifty years of age, he would readily have passed for a man of thirty. I will relate an instance, to confirm what I have said of his youthful appearance.

On one occasion, when he was in Europe, he was presented by the Minister of Foreign Affairs to

Bernadotte, king of Sweden. The king hesitated to address him, as he appeared to be so much younger than he expected. Bernadotte viewed him for a moment as if examining a recruit, but soon extended his hand, and said, in French: "Pardon me, sir; the gentleman the pleasure of whose call I was expecting I did not think to be younger than fifty or fifty-five years of age; and you, sir, do not look to be more than thirty, or thirty-five at most." After a pleasant exchange of compliments, the king proposed to sit on the sofa —a distinction, I believe, not often conferred at state presentations. Bernadotte spoke of having been selected by Napoleon to be Governor-General of Louisiana; but said the transfer of that province prevented him from acting in that capacity. "I examined," he continued, "the adjacent States, and am glad to see that the Kentuckians, who were to be my neighbors, have effected the improvements I contemplated."

Colonel Todd was much pleased with this reference to Kentucky. The king, then, asked about Mr. Monroe, and said that he had seen him in Paris. Bernadotte said, in this interview: "Mr. Monroe, I believe, appointed you minister to Colombia?" and, on being assured that he had, Bernadotte continued: "I have always been interested in South America, and will never cease to regret that their republics have not the stability of the United States."

In the conversation, which was prolonged for some time, the American Minister spoke of Louisiana forming one of the claims of the American Government to Oregon. The king said he hoped that Great Britain and the United States would not go to war about it.

CHAPTER XI.

Colonel Todd's Embarrassed Fortunes — His Personal Resemblance to Louis Philippe — Anecdote of that Monarch — Colonel Todd's Zeal for the Preservation of the Union — His Claim to a High Military Appointment in the Civil War acknowledged but not discharged — Evil Effects of Conferring Military Appointments on Civilians — Colonel Todd's Military Talents — He severs his Connection with the *Gazette.*

PERHAPS I ought not to forget to mention the great and successful efforts Colonel Todd made in freeing himself from his embarrassed fortunes, in early life, from the effects of a committal with a friend in trade, who died in the first year. He was called to manage a business for which he was not educated ; and, from the sudden revulsion of the times, by which real estate depreciated fifty to seventy-five per cent., he had to contend with an enormous debt for more than thirty years. He could have avoided it by taking the benefit of the Bankrupt law, but he resolved, even at the sacrifice of his domestic comfort, to go to the ends of the earth, if necessary, to become a free man. In this struggle, as in all other efforts, he was well sustained by the excellent sense and untiring energy of his devoted wife.

Colonel Todd, it is said, bore a strong personal likeness to Louis Philippe, king of France. I never saw the latter, and am, of course, unable to tell whether the resemblance was marked or not. I have heard, however, a story of Colonel Todd being taken for Louis Philippe as he was coming out of a theatre in Paris, where Rachel had been playing.

Some persons had seen Colonel Todd in the theatre, and taking him for the king, started the story that the king was there in disguise. Speaking of Louis Philippe reminds me of something Colonel Todd said about him. "I saw Louis Philippe," said the Colonel, "once or twice while in Europe, and I do not think that I have ever met a man of such a remarkable memory as he. Louis Philippe had been to this country, and seemed to remember everything he saw. On a visit to Lexington, Ky., he met a Miss Polly Todd, a belle and heiress of that place, and when I saw him in Europe, he inquired about her, and showed me how she used her fan, and described the quick and lively movement of her countenance. He also asked me about his landlord, Thomas, and about Bush, the hotel-keeper at Frankfort, Ky. Louis Philippe, in the same interview, spoke of the horrible taste of the salt and sulphur of the Blue Lick water, and said that the worst evil he wished his enemies was that they might be compelled to drink it."

When the war for the maintenance of the Union began, Colonel Todd was in Texas, and he hastened to Washington and offered his services to the country. The Administration, for some reason, did not give him an appointment. The Secretary of War said that he ought to have nothing less than a major-generalship; but he assigned as a reason for not giving the appointment, that the arrangement by which Secretary Cameron was sent to Russia, and the Hon. C. M. Clay given a major-generalship, had filled the quota of Kentucky. This treatment of Colonel Todd cannot well be overlooked. General Sherman said that he should be glad to serve under him ; and Col. O'Fallon, himself a gallant officer of the war of 1812, distinguished for gallantry at Tippecanoe, Fort Meigs, and at the battle of the Thames, earnestly and eloquently urged the Secretary to give some sort of position to Colonel Todd, by which the country could derive advantages from his military experience, &c. ; but the Secretary had taken his stand, and his decision was as irreversible as the laws of the Medes and Persians. The country learned too late the folly of appointing civilians and inexperienced soldiers to high military positions. It was one of the great'mistakes with which the war began, and it was kept up long after experience had shown how disastrous was its operation. Undoubtedly, it involved a terrible cost to the nation both in money and in life ; it protracted the war, and for years rendered the result doubtful ; it brought upon us nearly all of our defeats. If the absurd military ambition of politicians had been repressed or withstood ; if aspiring civilians, who never set a squadron in the field, had not, by unworthy influences upon public men too much subject to such influences, procured appointments to positions in which they weakly dreamed of hewing their way to the Presidency with their swords ; if men educated to war, and experienced in war, had been as fully relied on as they should have been, and in any other country would have been, to conduct the war, — the work which extended with constantly varying fortunes through nearly four years, would, in all probability, have been brought to a triumphant close in two ; and our country would now be enjoying all the blessings that a benignant heaven could bestow upon a grateful earth.

None who knew Colonel Todd can doubt that, in the war of the rebellion, he would, with fair opportunities, have achieved much for his country. His genius, his temperament, his deportment, his habits of thought, were decidedly and essentially military. He lacked no one of the qualities of a great commander — he possessed them all in an eminent degree. As knightly as any crusader that ever fought in Palestine, he was calm amid deadliest perils when calmness was needed, and as impetuous as a storm when impetuosity was demanded. In the field, he would never have failed in the fertility of his resources, or in the clearness, rapidity, and force of his strategic combinations. His great military powers improved by long and arduous service through all his life, and were disciplined by thoughtful and severe study. All the military authorities were familiar to him, and probably there is no volume upon the art of war that he would not have rendered more valuable by his comments.

Colonel Todd, in his civil and military service, adorned both, and he achieved victories in both. When he departed from among us, he probably did not leave a single peer behind.

In June, 1867, Colonel Todd, in a letter to me, thus refers to his proposed volume on the history of Kentucky:

" My Dear Sir : — Yesterday I prepared an introduction to the ‘ Sketches in the Early History of Kentucky,’ which I shall retain until I am able to prepare the first three or four chapters. Some of my friends here say that the *Gazette* is the best agricultural paper in the State. Let us

make it what it ought to be.   Address me at Shelbyville,
Ky., until Saturday.
   "Yours very truly,   C. S. Todd."

A few weeks after I received this letter, Colonel
Todd notified me that he intended to resign his position on the *Gazette*, on account of his being compelled
to be absent so much from the city.   .

In a few weeks after Colonel Todd's resignation,
I also severed my connection with the paper.   The
old association was broken up.   I had no longer a
staff to lean upon, and my work became neither
pleasant nor profitable to me.

CHAPTER XII.

Colonel Todd's Friendship for the Author — His Opinion of Actors and
Acting — His Exalted Estimate of the Character of Dr. Theodore S.
Bell — A Letter to the Author — Colonel Todd's Address before the
Perry Monument Association — Friendship between Colonel Todd and
the Hon. J. Scott Harrison.

COLONEL TODD enjoyed excellent health up
to the time of his last illness.   He took a
deep interest in my literary career, and always complimented me by asking my opinion of his own articles.
When absent from Louisville he wrote me almost
every week.   I give below an extract from a letter,
dated May 18th, 1868: "We had a pleasant trip
on the steamer to New Orleans.   Mr. —— was a
passenger, and met me with great cordiality, and
tried to talk to me about his paper, and asked me if

18

I knew the present editor; but I waived the whole subject. I wish my business arrangements would allow me to see Mr. Draper, the historian, at your house. Remember me kindly to him, and your poet wife, who will greatly enjoy his company."

In February, 1869, he wrote: "I am gratified by the opinion you express as to General Grant. He will make the best President we have had since the days of Washington. I think you ought to hesitate long before you invest money in a newspaper. I am glad you have such confidence in Dr. Gross, of Philadelphia. I wish for you the very best results from his treatment. I trust Mr. Prentice is well; his verses to sweet Virgiline are exquisitely beautiful. By the way, I should like you to read Mr. Maxwell's book entitled 'The Czar — His Court and People.' It contains an account, also, of Norway and Sweden, which he visited in 1844. You ask me what I think of Prescott. You know my opinion of Mr. Motley; and I am at a loss to tell which is the greater of the two."

A few weeks later he wrote: "I have just read your article on Mrs. Prentice. She is credited with higher accomplishments than I thought she possessed. Her father was a very able advocate. I saw Mrs. Prentice a very short time after her marriage, and I thought her very beautiful."

"I am flattered," he wrote me, still later "with your opinion of my brief article on Jackson's Battle Ground. I have a very interesting letter from Dr. Usher Parsons, Perry's surgeon, eighty years old, thanking me for some military sketches I sent him at Providence, R. I. I will bring it with me when I come to Louisville."

In speaking of actors and acting, Colonel Todd said : "I do not go to the theatre; but I take a great interest in the drama, and often find myself reading even the gossip about the players, that have been well called the 'abstract and brief chroniclers of the time.'" In a postscript to this letter he added : " Do not think I have written the above for an excuse to praise your article on Booth's Iago, which, by the way, is the best thing I have seen from your pen ; but, to tell you candidly, I have always taken an interest in such things."

Of Dr. T. S. Bell he said : " I have always, though personally unknown to Dr. Bell, cherished the most exalted estimate of his character."

The following letter I print entire, as it shows the pains Colonel Todd took in preparing his essay on the Battle of the Thames, to which I have before referred :

" OWENSBOROUGH, 6th December, '67.

"Accept my thanks for your kind letter of the 4th instant ; and while I am greatly flattered by your opinion of the second number of the Battle of the Thames, I had hoped the first number was acceptable,— please to excuse my jealousy. The third number is postponed until next week, by a part of the manuscript being misplaced in the office. It consists chiefly of an extract of General Harrison's official letter as to the conduct of his officers and men ; a criticism by Major Wood ; Mr. Madison's report to Congress, and their vote of thanks, and medals, &c., with a neat commentary by Ritchie, of the *Richmond Enquirer.* I hope it may meet your expectations, and that, *as a whole,* the article will command the attention of the descendants of the disinterested patriots on that great occasion.

" I have taken occasion to dwell on the merits of Major Wood, who was breveted lieutenant-colonel for gallantry in the Battle of Lundy's Lane, 25th July, 1814; and General Brown did himself great honor in reporting to the Government that he owed the safety of his army to Colonels McKee and Wood more than to any other officers in his army. My notice of his heroic career is but a feeble expression of my gratitude to him for once saving my life."

In September, 1864, Colonel Todd was invited to deliver the Annual Address before the Perry Monument Association, composed of the surviving soldiers of the war of 1812, at Put-in-Bay Island, on the victory of Lake Erie, September, 1813. This address was the best public speech he ever made. The following is the concluding paragraph.

"And now, venerated friends, let us rejoice that we have been permitted once more to celebrate the most memorable event in the heroic period of the country, the second war of Independence, which aided essentially in making us a commanding power among the nations of the earth. It developed our resources in agriculture, in internal communication, in minerals (especially of iron and coal so necessary to a manufacturing people), in a commerce whitening every sea. The generations which have grown up since that war should know that the war of the Revolution led to separation from the mother country, while the war of 1812 was a war for our nationality. Dr. Franklin said that the war of the colonies was a revolution, but the war of real independence was yet to come. The prophecy of the great philosopher and statesman was fulfilled in our successful struggle in 1812–15."

About the time Colonel Todd delivered this address, he wrote me: "I have received the enclosed beautiful letter from my friend, Mr. Yeaman, the minister to Denmark. In it you will see how Bis-

marck speaks of his old schoolmate. Give my regards
to our excellent friend, Dr. Bell, by whom I shall stand
in every emergency. I have read his reply to Gail-
lard. It is a masterpiece of criticism."

In October, 1869, he wrote : " I wish that you would
write something about the Hon. J. Scott Harrison.
He is the only surviving son of General Harrison,
and he ought to have charge and possession of the
grounds and remains for a monument. I am anxious
to hear from Mr. Motley."

The warmest feelings of personal friendship existed
between Colonel Todd and the Hon. J. Scott Harrison.
Colonel Todd never heard Mr. Harrison's name
mentioned without saying something in his praise.
The subjoined extract from a letter written to Colonel Todd shows how Mr. Harrison reciprocated the
friendly feeling:

" COLONEL C. S. TODD.

" MY DEAR SIR: — Your criticisms on the Northwestern
campaign of the war of 1812 are in generous accord with
that zealous devotion so often manifested before in the defence of my father's military reputation, and for which the
surviving members have ever felt the deepest gratitude. It
has always been a sense of great regret to me that my
father did not live long enough after his official exaltation
to manifest to the nation and the world — in a more
emphatic way than he ever before had opportunity — his
high appreciation of the gallantry and services of those
noble officers and men who served with him in his arduous
campaign ; and whose valuable services have never yet
been fully appreciated, either by Congress or the American
people. I need not say, my dear sir, that (in my father's
estimation) *you* stood pre-eminently distinguished among
these devoted heroes.   J. SCOTT HARRISON."

When Colonel Todd's name was brought before the President as a suitable person to represent the country abroad, Mr. Harrison wrote:

" I cannot close this communication without expressing to you the deep anxiety our family feel for the successful termination of Colonel Todd's application. My mother, particularly, would feel great pleasure in seeing this true and devoted friend of her lamented husband placed in a situation that would relieve him from embarrassment, and feel that he had not been neglected by that country he served so early and so faithfully. You may be assured that Colonel Todd has a strong hold on the affections of the people of the West; they know him as the youthful but gallant soldier of the last war, as well as the confidential friend and supporter of their General in the conflict which has just ended ; which contest, though less bloody, was equally as vindictive and proscriptive toward their favorite chief. I hope you will pardon this liberty. I was emboldened by your friendly request to communicate my wishes freely.

" With my best wishes for your successful administration of the Government, I remain, with sentiments of high respect and friendly consideration,

J. SCOTT HARRISON."

CHAPTER XIII.

Letter from the Hon. William C. Rives to Colonel Todd — Colonel Todd prepares Several Articles for Dr. Sprague's "National Portrait Gallery"— Dr. Sprague's Acknowledgments — Governor Shelby's Pride in Colonel Todd — Colonel Todd's Last Illness — His Death.

THE HON. WILLIAM C. RIVES, of Virginia, often consulted Colonel Todd upon state affairs. I introduce here a letter from Mr. Rives, which not only expresses the confidence he felt in Colonel Todd's friendship, but in his judgment and ability.

"CASTLE HILL, 18th January, 1848.

" MY DEAR SIR : — It gives me great pleasure, I assure you, to hear from you, as renewing the impressions of an early friendship, which I have been most happy to cherish through all the vicissitudes of my life.

" I rejoice with you in the great event which has delivered us from the reign of folly and madness in our public councils, and opens to the country a new future bright with hope and the promise of a noble destiny. I have not the satisfaction, as you doubtless have, of a personal acquaintance with the illustrious character whom the nation has called to its head; but I have formed the highest opinion of his wisdom, moderation, and patriotism; and I look with entire confidence to his administration to restore the earlier and better days of the Republic.

" I am very sensible, my dear sir, of your partiality and kindness in wishing to see me again called into the public service. I have long considered this a matter of so much uncertainty that I have formed no particular wishes on the subject, but readily conform to whatever the course of events brings along with it, as marking both the path of duty and inclination for me.

"Wishing you every prosperity both in private and public life, and assuring you of the pleasure it will give me at all times to hear from you,

"I remain, very truly and faithfully, your friend,

"CHAS. S. TODD, ESQ.   W. C. RIVES."

In October, of the same year of the date of the above letter, Colonel Todd prepared several articles for Dr. W. B. Sprague's great work, entitled "The National Portrait Gallery." One of these articles consists of a carefully written biographical essay on Governor Isaac Shelby. The annexed letter from Dr. Sprague expresses his thanks to Colonel Todd for the same, and for the interest he had taken in the work:

"ALBANY, October 19th, 1849.

"MY DEAR COLONEL:—Your most welcome and gratifying communications have come safely to hand, and I cannot tell you how much I feel obliged for them. Besides containing beautiful and, I doubt not, faithful sketches of your two distinguished friends, they secure to my work the influence of your own name, and to me the gratification of being associated with you in what to me is a very favorite enterprise. You will be glad to hear that your friend, ex-President Tyler, has also given me his recollections of Bishop Madison, in a very neat and highly graphic communication. Many thanks for the Bishop's letter. It was a precious morsel to my 'omnivorous' appetite.

"My family join me in kindest regards to you, and I am, my dear sir, with the highest regard, faithfully and gratefully yours,   W. B. SPRAGUE."

Governor Shelby was very proud of his son-in-law, Colonel Todd, and did not fail to consult him about national affairs and the relations of private life. I have, since writing the above, found an unpublished letter from Governor Shelby to Colonel Todd, dated December 19, 1818. It is expressive of the wise judgment and sagacity of that distinguished military chieftain. This letter was written at Traveller's Rest, the beautiful home of Governor Shelby.

"The Secretary of War is much pleased with the Chickasaw treaty; it is most probable you will soon hear of its ratification by the Senate. The Legislature should be prepared to act upon it very promptly; this is certainly a favorable moment to settle the question of boundary between the two States whose interests seem to invite a renewal of the discussions on the subject; it is one that has been long at issue, and for fifty years back engrossed the minds of the wisest men on the Western waters. If it is renewed, in terms of delicacy and conciliation, I have no doubt it may be settled, although it is a question on which the people of Tennessee are very tenacious, and would be easily roused to desperation. If this occasion is passed over, it may not be settled in another half-century of years. I hope the Assembly will take care to guard the lands west of the Tennessee river from all unjust claims; it is the last stake we have to accomplish any great public purpose. Those lands, if rightly appropriated, would clear the falls of the Ohio; or cut a canal around them, and make a turnpike way from the gap of Cumberland mountain to Louisville. If this Assembly suffers that fund to slip through their hands, they should be execrated forever and forever."

A short memoir of Governor Shelby will be found in the Appendix to this volume.

In the last letter Colonel Todd wrote me, he said: "I regret that you have incurred the ill-will of W—— and R——. The truth is, they look upon you as a rising man, and want to put you down. You must not be intimidated. Their unkind feelings proceed from something out of joint in themselves.

19

You could not have given them any just cause for such treatment. Jealousy is at the bottom of it. If I am spared long enough, I shall help you make them regret their course."

I wrote to my dear old friend several times after the receipt of the above, but no answer came to me. I began to fear that he was ill. I thought of his advanced age, and felt that I should never see him again in this world. I knew that he expected soon to come to Louisville, and was cheered with the hope that he did not write because he expected so soon to be with me. He left New Orleans for a visit to his grand - daughter's at Baton Rouge. The weather was so pleasant that he would not listen to the advice of one of his children to put on his great-coat, and the result was that he took a severe cold, which was followed by a severe attack of pneumonia, from which he never recovered.

A few days before his death he called his daughter, Mrs. Letitia Carter, wife of Dr. John Carter, of New Orleans, La., to his bed-side, and asked her to find the psalm which says, "Thy rod and thy staff they comfort me." She turned to the chapter containing it, and asked him if she should read it, when he said that he wished it for a reference only. On the Tuesday before he died, he said to his physician: "I trust, Doctor, that I shall go quietly;" and then, addressing Mrs. Carter, said, "Let me, my precious child, feel the pressure of your hand when my spirit is about to take its flight." It was then ten o'clock in the evening. He continued to grow worse, and, while struggling to utter some loving word to those around him, his noble spirit took its flight to its home beyond the skies.

APPENDIX.

Correspondence of Colonel Todd with the Colombian General Santander —
Memoir of Governor Shelby.

BOGOTA, June 1st, 1823.

THE Undersigned, Colonel C. S. Todd, presents his most respectful compliments to his Excellency, General Santander, and begs leave, informally and unofficially, as a citizen of the first Republic of the North, animated by the most anxious solicitude, to omit no occasion of promoting a frank and cordial intercourse between Colombia and the United States; and, to avoid every measure calculated in the slightest degree to interrupt the most perfect harmony between them, to submit to a distinguished citizen of the first Republic of the South the following statement and correspondence, in the firm persuasion that he addresses himself to an individual whose character may be found in the great qualities of valor in the field, uniform and patriotic devotion to the best interests of his country, a display of practical wisdom in the civil administration, and who, loving "Colombia first and Colombia last," has been signalized by the maintenance of feelings of justice and impartiality towards all nations.

The enclosed document, No. 1, consists of a translation of the Commission granted to the Undersigned by the Government of the United States, on the 20th April, 1820, of the correspondence, which, by virtue of that instrument and his instructions, he had the honor of instituting with the authorities of Colombia, from the 2d August, 1820, to the 15th February, 1821, and of sundry extracts. These papers are communicated now in consequence of the Undersigned having lately received information from a

147

most respectable source that they were not made known
to the Congress at Cucata, and therefore they may possibly
be still unknown to his Excellency General Santander.

The Undersigned has been further informed, on the same
authority, of the great probability that the discrimination
in the law of the 25th September, 1821, unfavorable to the
commerce of the United States, would not have been
adopted, if the views, acts, and feelings of the Government
of the United States conveyed in these documents had
been communicated to that Congress. The Undersigned
positively states, that his letter of the 2d August, 1820, was
received by the Government of Augostura in the following
September; and that his letter of the 25th February, 1821,
with its enclosures, was delivered prior to the 3d of May,
and thereafter to General Narino, then at Cucata, and President of Colombia. He is greatly concerned to be obliged,
from a sense of duty to the United States, to state his belief
that the existence of the mission with which he was intrusted
by his Government, and of this letter of the 15th February,
1821, was known to the present Secretary of State for
Foreign Affairs, who was a member of that Congress, and
one of the projectors and supporters of the particular article
in the law of the 25th September, not less prejudicial to the
real interests of Colombia than those of the United States.
If, as is positively asserted to have been the case, papers
transmitting intelligence of events and circumstances so
interesting to the Congress and people of Colombia, were
withheld by the Executive and the particular department
charged with foreign affairs, at a period when the false
representations were industriously circulated to the injury
of the United States concerning their acts and feelings,
and whilst a law was enacted imposing a discrimination
unfavorable to their commerce, His Excellency General
Santander cannot be surprised that the Undersigned should
suspect him to be still unadvised of the proceedings as well
as of the precise import of other transactions to which the
Undersigned will have occasion presently to refer.

It is respectfully submitted to the enlightened judgment
and honorable views of his Excellency General Santander,
to say what would be the impression produced on his
mind, if, under such circumstances, the Congress of any
foreign nation were to proceed from unfriendly opinions
to hostile legislative acts towards Colombia — at a precise
period when the Executive, or one of its subordinate
officers, withheld from their knowledge official documents
that would have removed these unfavorable feelings and
consequently the law founded on them. In this case, an
impression generally prevailed among the members of the
Congress at Cucata, that, in the late treaty acquiring possession of the Floridas, the United States agreed not to recognize
the independence of any of the new governments in South
America ; whilst an examination of the letter of the Undersigned with its enclosures, dated on the 2d August, 1820,
would have shown what had been previously published to
the world, that the Government of the United States, so far
from acceding to so odious a stipulation, considered it impossible to discuss a proposition so incompatible with their
honor and independence.

Deeply as the Undersigned regretted, at the time, the
necessity which the alarming state of his health imposed
on him of returning to the United States in February, 1821,
the knowledge lately acquired of the extraordinary direction given to his correspondence, and the numerous baneful impressions which were then falsely and maliciously
suggested and permitted respecting the acts and feelings
of a sister republic, induce him now to lament, that his
absence afforded an opportunity for the enemies of both
republics to infuse these prejudices into the minds of the
members of that Congress; and if, in the course of his
present mission, he shall be enabled, by removing the
effects of misrepresentation, to place the relations of the
two countries where they should be, on a footing of the
most intimate and unreserved cordiality, he shall regard
the effort with the proudest recollection.

The Undersigned regrets that any combination of circumstances should impose on him the painful necessity of appearing to give explanations with regard to the acts and views of his Government, whose attitude towards this country is so pure and magnanimous ; but the sincere desire he cherishes for the preservation of perpetual harmony between the two republics requires of him to contribute his efforts toward removing the seeds of future collisions between them. The conduct of the United States has been open to the World, and cannot be misunderstood but through the machinations of those whose passions and interests may lead them to misrepresent it. With regard to the struggle for independence in the South, their course has been that of deep sympathy in favor of their oppressed brethren ; and, although they have not participated directly in the war, their system of neutrality has entirely satisfied the wishes of the true friends of both countries. The misrepresentations of this conduct, which have been circulated for several years in Colombia, chiefly from the want of correct information, will be a sufficient apology for the Undersigned in claiming the attention of his Excellency General Santander ; whilst he briefly reviews the several acts and declarations of his government in relation to the interesting struggle in South America. He has the honor of referring to an extract of the Message of the President of the United States in December, 1811, and the report of the committee of that Congress, translations of which are herewith enclosed, containing a beautiful and enlightened allusion to the interest the Government and people of the United States should feel in the welfare of their Southern brethren. During that session a very generous and timely supply of one hundred thousand dollars, in provisions, was voted to relieve the distresses of the people of Venezuela, occasioned by the earthquakes of March, 1812, — a supply denied them by the authorities of the adjacent islands. The war, which the rights and honor of the United States compelled that Congress to declare against the same Power whose cruelties and oppressions led to the war of the Revolution, and made them free and independent States, necessarily engaged the exclusive attention of the Government and people of the United States; and it was not, therefore, to be expected that, in the midst of its difficulties, any particular notice could be taken of the progress of the South American contest. It may be, perhaps, deemed unnecessary here to remind his Excellency General Santander of the distinguished reputation acquired by the United States in that portentous struggle for the preservation of their liberties; but the Undersigned cannot resist the suggestions of a just pride in stating, that every portion of the civilized world has resounded with the imposing and animating facts that a handful of Republicans, after a peace of thirty years, triumphed in a war of less than three years over the veteran forces of an empire which claimed dominion in every quarter of the globe; that, though Great Britain had all the influence of the moral power of the States, with the exception of France, composing the present " Holy Alliance," aided by that of Spain and Portugal, the United States came out of the contest with their rights asserted, their national resources developed, and their national character exalted; that the sacrifices encountered and the energies successfully displayed promise them a long harvest of peace — the natural state and essential policy of all republics; that, in the course of this momentous struggle, that gallant navy, which had been contemptuously styled " a few fir-built frigates with a piece of striped bunting at the masthead," by its daring chivalric deeds, with inferior force, repeatedly · humbled the pride of the leviathan of the deep, who, after a thousand victories over the fleets of Europe, had arrogantly assumed to be " mistress of the seas;" that this same valorous spirit led to the capture with inferior force of whole squadrons on the inland seas which skirt our frontiers; that our armies, as if inspired with the energy and sublimity of the mighty cataract in their vicinity, had routed British veteran troops in open combat at the point of the

bayonet ; and that, finally, on the plains of New Orleans, a
few undisciplined freemen, with the impetuosity of the
floods of their own Mississippi, proudly repelled the bar-
barian invasion of the "conquerors of the conquerors of
Europe." It is these moral energies of a free people in a
just cause which the tyrants of Europe so much dread, and
the display of which gives us, for the present, the blessings
of peace.

The Undersigned begs leave to refer to the enclosed
translations of extracts of the messages of the President
of the United States to Congress on the opening of the
sessions, in December, 1817, 1818, 1819, and 1820, and to
state that, while the Executive Department was evincing
its lively interest in the course of events in South America
by these public declarations, and the appointment of the
Undersigned on the 20th April, 1820, to maintain informally
commercial and political relations with the Government of
Colombia, the popular branch of the Legislative Department solemnly avowed, in 1820 and in 1821, its wishes in
behalf of their struggling brethren, and its readiness to
unite with the Executive in instituting with the new governments in South America all the relations incident to
free and independent States. It is thus seen, that, long
before 1822, the applications of the Government of Colombia, to be practically recognized by the United States, had
been acceded to by the adoption of the public acts and
declarations just referred to ; and the records of the Supreme
Court of the United States will show, also, that the flag of
Buenos Ayres and Carthagena was regarded as legal, as
early as 1815, in consequence of the declarations made by
the President of the United States that the Government of
the United States viewed the contest not as a rebellion or
insurrection, but as a civil war entitling each party to equal
rights in their ports. And here the Undersigned would
beg leave most respectfully to inquire whether, until the
last year, the head or supreme authorities of any other
nation have considered the Government of Colombia to be

of such importance as to induce them, by their public acts
and declarations, to proclaim to the world the existence of
a struggle for liberty on this continent? So far from adopting a course so magnanimous and so animating to the
"moral march of its affairs," if it has even been noticed,
it has been merely to refer to their wishes for the restora-
tion of the authority of Spain over her rebellious and
insurgent subjects; nor can it be doubted that the formal
recognition by the United States of the Government of
Colombia, in April, 1822, had a powerful influence in causing
its flag to be subsequently acknowledged in the ports of
France, Great Britain, Sweden, Denmark, Holland, and
Portugal.

In illustration of the acts and views of the United States
in 1818 and 1819, the Undersigned encloses, also, extracts
of the instructions to Commodore Perry, dated in May,
1819, and made part of his instructions; and, as an evidence of his frank and confiding disposition in the kind
feelings of his Excellency General Santander, he com-
municates an extract of a confidential conversation with
the President of the United States after the return of the
Undersigned to the United States in 1821.

The Undersigned, having no information of an official
translator being employed in this capital, and to avoid
the consequences which might flow from possible miscon-
ceptions of his acts and correspondence, has the honor of
submitting (in document No. 2) a translation of all the communications he has addressed to the Secretary of Foreign
Affairs, since his arrival in this city, on the several subjects
noticed in his instructions and in the enclosed letter from
the Secretary of State of the United States. In the note
of the Undersigned on the 28th May last, his Excellency
General Santander will find a review of the ineffectual
efforts made by him to procure an adjustment of those
cases of claims acknowledged to be due or not contro-
verted. The omission of the Secretary, even to notice these
applications, renders it improper, under existing circum-

20

stances, for the Undersigned to renew the subject to this government through that channel. A sense of self-respect, as well as of the regard due to the dignity of the United States, will not permit him to adopt a measure of such condescension.

In addressing himself thus informally and unofficially, though in direct terms, to his Excellency General Santander, the Undersigned is persuaded that he appeals to a common friend of North and South America, who will unite with him in removing those impressions which, under the influence of evil persons equally hostile to the best interests of both republics, might eventually ripen into jealousies, and disturb the harmony which a thousand interesting considerations, at this period, make it the duty of both governments to preserve. The Undersigned, in requesting his Excellency General Santander to interpose his influence in relieving him from the painful dilemma to which the most extraordinary and unjustifiable views have reduced his official relations with this Government, might appeal to the kindred blood, which has flowed in this cause, in the sacrifice of Macauley, Donohue, and a hundred other gallant Americans ; to the enterprising efforts of American merchants at the most critical periods of the Revolution, among which cases incidentally known to the Undersigned, as constituting still unsatisfied claims for upwards of six hundred thousand dollars, may be estimated the fortunate supplies lately furnished at Carthagena, at La Guira, in the acquisition of the ship "Bolivar," proudly regarded as a terror to her enemies, and more especially to the timely supply made to General Bolivar, at Augostura, in 1819, when, it is believed, he had not more than twenty-five muskets, with which supply he restored this capital and New Granada to the Republic, and covered himself and all concerned, particularly his Excellency General Santander, with immortal glory in the memorable battle of Boyaca. But the Undersigned appeals to still higher motives. He appeals to the common principles on which the two Republics have been erected on the same continent after a similar struggle to maintain their sacred rights; to the common interests which, as neighbors, unite them in the bonds of reciprocal commerce, and more especially to the political motives which make it the imperious duty of all the governments on continental America to cultivate the best understanding, that they may be prepared to counteract the designs of that foul confederacy of kings in Europe, created for the purpose of sacrificing the rights of the many to the aggrandizement of the few; which, prostrating in its march of desolation every vestige of civilization and of human rights in the Old World, may seek in the New to crush those generous displays which have signalized the people of the South in their imitation of the "first successful effort of democratic rebellion" in the North.

In presenting himself thus frankly and fully to his Excellency General Santander, the Undersigned indulges in the pleasing hope that he affords conclusive evidence ·of his deep solicitude for the prosperity of both republics — a solicitude, which, in the midst of domestic sacrifices and exposures of health, can never be remunerated, has induced him to persevere, for the last years, in the most faithful efforts to bring the two Governments into a just appreciation of their mutual friendship and interests.

The Undersigned avails himself of the occasion to tender assurances of the high respect with which he has the honor to be his Excellency's

Very obedient servant,   C. S. TODD.

HIS EXCELLENCY GENERAL SANTANDER.

June 14, 1823.

Whilst translations of the preceding statement and documents were preparing, the Undersigned received, on the 5th instant, a letter from the Secretary of Foreign Affairs in relation to the claims noticed in his notes of the 12th and 28th May. This reply would seem, on first impression, to obviate the necessity, in part, of resorting to the measure

deemed indispensable to a right understanding of all the
circumstances connected with an harmonious intercourse
between the two countries. But without adverting to the
possibility that the conversation between the Undersigned
and his distinguished informants already referred to may
have hastened the receipt of this reply by the Secretary of
Foreign Affairs, the Undersigned, on mature consideration,
has concluded to persevere in his original purpose of presenting to his Excellency General Santander the statement
and documents in the precise shape in which they were
prepared, persuaded, as he is, that his Excellency General
Santander will concur, in the hope and belief that full, free,
and frank explanations cannot fail to have the happy
tendency of removing *radically* all sources of future mis-
understanding, and of laying the foundation of the most
unreserved cordiality in the future intercourse between the
two republics. To effectuate such a high and permanent
object, the Undersigned disregards all personal considerations in the firm conviction that he will be sustained in
his course by the enlightened and liberal feelings of both
Governments ; and this entire exposition is made, now,
with the view of advising his Excellency General Santander
of the crisis to which these circumstances were rapidly precipitating the official relations between the two countries ;
it will thus stand as a beacon to warn the agents of both
Governments against the baneful consequences likely to
flow from a similar controversy. In this gratifying hope,
and that this statement may be reviewed in the same spirit
of liberal friendship in which it is transmitted, the Undersigned dismisses the subject by forwarding a translation of
his reply of this date to the Secretary of Foreign Affairs,
and repeating the assurance of his distinguished consideration.   C. S. TODD.

MEMOIR OF GOVERNOR SHELBY.

I SAAC SHELBY, the subject of this memoir, was born on the 11th day of December, 1750, near to the North Mountain, a few miles from Hagerstown, in Maryland, where his father and grandfather settled after their arrival in America from Wales. In that early settlement of the country, which was annoyed during the period of his youth by Indian wars, he obtained only the elements of a plain English education ; but, like his father General Evan Shelby, born with a strong constitution, capable of bearing great privation and fatigue, he was brought up to the use of arms and the pursuit of game.

At the age of twenty-one, he took up his residence in Western Virginia, beyond the Alleghany Mountains, having previously acquired a knowledge of surveying and of the duties of sheriff at Fredericktown. He was engaged, in his new residence, in the business of feeding and attending to herds of cattle in the extensive range which distinguished that section of country. He was a lieutenant in the company of his father, the late General Evan Shelby, in the memorable battle fought 10th of October, 1774, at the mouth of the Kenhawa, at the close of which his father was the commanding officer, Colonels Lewis, Fleming, and Field having been killed or disabled. The result of this battle gave peace to the frontier, at the critical period of the Colonies venturing into the eventful contest of the revolution, and deterred the Indians from uniting with the British until 1776. This was, probably, the most severely contested conflict ever maintained with the Northwestern Indians ; the action continued from sunrise to sunset, and the ground, for half a mile along the bank of the Ohio, was alternately occupied by each of the parties in the course of the day. So sanguinary was the contest, that blood was found on each

side of the trees behind which the parties were posted.
The Indians, under the celebrated chief Cornstalk, abandoned
the ground under cover of the night. Their loss, according
to the official report, exceeded that of the Americans; the
latter amounting to sixty-three killed and eighty wounded.
This report was drawn up by Captain Russell, reputed to be
the best scholar in camp, and the father of the late Colonel
William Russell, of Kentucky. The fortune of the day, as
stated in Doddridge's notes of " Border War," was decided
by a bold movement to the rear of the left wing of the
Indians, led by Captain Evan Shelby, in which the subject
of this memoir bore a conspicuous part.

The garrison at Kenhawa was commanded by Captain
Russell, and Lieutenant Shelby continued in it until the
troops were disbanded in July, 1775, by order of Governor
Dunmore, who was apprehensive that the post might be
held for the benefit of the rebel authorities. He proceeded
immediately to Kentucky, and was employed as a surveyor
under Henderson & Co., who styled themselves proprietors
of the country, and who had established a regular land-
office under their purchase from the Cherokees. He
resided in the then wilderness of Kentucky for nearly
twelve months, and, being without bread or salt, he returned home.

In July, 1776, during his absence from home, he was
appointed captain of a minute company by the committee
of safety of Virginia. In the year of 1777 he was appointed
by Governor Henry a commissary of supplies for an extensive body of militia, posted at different garrisons to
guard the frontier settlements, and for a treaty to be held
at the Long Island of Holston river with the Cherokee tribe
of Indians. These supplies could not have been obtained
nearer than Staunton, Va., a distance of three hundred
miles; but by the most indefatigable perseverance (one of
the most conspicuous traits of his character) he accomplished it to the satisfaction of his country.

In 1778, he was engaged in the commissary department,

providing supplies for the Continental army and for an
expedition, by the way of Pittsburg, against the Northwestern Indians.   In the early part of 1779, he was appointed,
by Governor Henry, to furnish supplies for the campaign
against the Chicamauga Indians, which he effected upon
his own individual credit.   In the spring of that year he was
elected a member of the Virginia Legislature from Washington County ; and in the fall of that year was commissioned
a major, by Governor Jefferson, in the escort of guards to
the commissioners for extending the boundary line between
this State and North Carolina.   By the extension of that
line his residence was found to be within the limits of the
latter' State, and shortly afterwards he was appointed by
Governor Caswell a colonel of the new county of Sullivan,
established in consequence of the additional territory acquired by the securing of that line.

    In the summer of 1780 Colonel Shelby was in Kentucky,
locating and securing those lands which he had five years
previously marked out and improved for himself, when the
intelligence of the surrender of Charleston, and the loss of
the army, reached that country.   He returned home in July
of that year, determined to enter the service of his country,
and remain in it until her independence should be secured.
He could not continue to be a cool spectator of a contest
in which the dearest rights and interests of his country
were involved.   On his arrival in Sullivan, he found a
requisition from General Charles McDowell, requesting
him to furnish all the aid in his power to check the enemy,
who had overrun the two Southern States, and were on the
borders of North Carolina.   Colonel Shelby assembled the
militia of his county, called upon them to volunteer their
services for a short time on that interesting occasion, and
marched, in a few days, with three hundred mounted riflemen across the Alleghany Mountains.

    In a short time after his arrival at McDowell's Camp,
near the Cherokee Ford of Broad River, Colonel Shelby and
Lieutenant-Colonels Sevin and Clarke, the latter a refugee

officer from Georgia, were detached with six hundred men to surprise a post of the enemy, in front, on the waters of Pacolet river. It was a strong fort, surrounded by abattis, built in the Cherokee war, and commanded by that distinguished loyalist, Captain Patrick Moore, who surrendered the garrison with one British sergeant-major, ninety-three loyalists, and two hundred and fifty stand of arms. Major Ferguson, of the British army, though a brigadier-general in the royal militia, and the most distinguished partisan officer in the British army, made many ineffectual efforts to surprise Colonel Shelby. His advance, about six or seven hundred strong, came up with the American commander at Cedar Spring, and, before Ferguson approached with his whole force, the Americans took two officers and fifty men prisoners, and safely effected their retreat. It was in the severest part of this action that Colonel Shelby's attention was arrested by the heroic conduct of Colonel Clarke. He often mentioned the circumstance of his ceasing in the midst of the battle to look with astonishment and admiration at Clarke's fighting.

The next important event was the battle fought at Musgrove's Mill, on the south side of the Enoree river, distant forty miles, with seven hundred men, led by Colonels Shelby, Clarke, and Williams, of South Carolina. This affair took place on the 19th of August, and is more particularly described in the sketch of Colonel Shelby, inserted in the first volume of the "National Portrait Gallery," published in 1834 under the direction of the American Academy of Fine Arts. It has been introduced into the historical romance called "Horse-Shoe Robinson," and noticed, also, in McCall's "History of Georgia," where the British loss is stated to be sixty-three killed and one hundred and sixty wounded and taken; the American loss four killed and nine wounded, — among the former Captain Inman, and among the latter Colonel Clarke and Captain Clarke. Colonel Innes, the British commander of the "Queen's American Regiment," from New York, was wounded; and all the

British officers, except a subaltern, were killed or wounded; and Captain Hawsey, a noted leader among the Tories, was killed. The Americans intended to be, that evening, before Ninety-six; but at that moment an express from General McDowell came up, in great haste, with a short note from Governor Caswell, dated on the battle-ground, apprising McDowell of the defeat of the American grand army, under General Gates, on the 16th, near Camden. Fortunately, Colonel Shelby knew Caswell's handwriting, and by distributing the prisoners among the companies so as to make one to every three men, who carried them alternately on horseback, the detachment moved directly toward the mountains. The Americans were saved by a long and rapid march that day and night, and until the evening of the next day, without halting to refresh. Colonel Shelby, after seeing the party and prisoners out of danger, retreated to the Western waters, and left the prisoners in the charge of Clarke and Williams, to convey them to a place of safety in Virginia; for at that moment there was no corps of Americans south of that State. The brilliancy of this affair was obscured, as indeed were all the minor events of the previous war, by the deep gloom which overspread the public mind after the disastrous defeat of General Gates.

Ferguson was so solicitous to recapture the prisoners, and to check these daring adventures of the mountaineers, that he made a strenuous effort, with his main body, to intercept them; but failing of his object, he took post at a place called Gilberttown, from whence he sent the most threatening messages by paroled prisoners to the officers west of the mountains, proclaiming devastation to their country if they did not cease their opposition to the British Government.

This was the most disastrous and critical period of the revolutionary war to the South. No one could see whence a force could be raised to check the enemy in their progress to subjugate this portion of the continent.

21

Cornwallis, with the main army, was posted at Charlotte-town in North Carolina, and Ferguson, with three thousand, at Gilberttown; while many of the best friends of the American Government, despairing of the freedom and independence of America, took protection under the British standard. At this gloomy moment, Colonel Shelby proposed to Colonels Sevin and Campbell to raise a force from their several counties, march hastily through the mountains, and attack and surprise Ferguson in the night. Accordingly, they collected with their followers, about one thousand strong, on Doe Run, in the spurs of the Alleghany, on the 25th of September, 1780, and the next day commenced their march, when it was discovered that three of Colonel Sevin's men had deserted to the enemy. This disconcerted their first design, and induced them to turn to the left, gain his front, and act as events might suggest. They travelled through mountains almost inaccessible to horsemen. As soon as they entered the level country, they met with Colonel Cleveland with three hundred men, and with Colonels Williams and Lacy, and other refugee officers, who had heard of Cleveland's advance, by which three hundred more were added to the mountaineers. They now considered themselves to be sufficiently strong to encounter Ferguson; but being rather a confused mass, without any head, it was proposed by Colonel Shelby in a council of officers, and agreed to, that Colonel Campbell, of the Virginia Regiment, — an officer of enterprise, patriotism, and good sense, — should be appointed to the command. And having determined to pursue Ferguson, with all practicable dispatch, two nights before the action, they selected the best horses and rifles, and at the dawn of day commenced their march with nine hundred and ten expert marksmen. As Ferguson was their object, they would not be diverted from the main point by any collection of Tories in the vicinity of their route. They had pursued him for the last thirty-six hours without alighting from their horses to refresh but once — at the Cowpens — for an hour, although the day of the action was so extremely wet that the men could only keep their guns dry by wrapping their bags, blankets, and hunting-shirts around the locks, which exposed their bodies to a heavy and incessant rain during the pursuit.

By the order of march and of battle, Colonel Campbell's regiment formed the right, and Colonel Shelby's regiment the left column, in the centre ; the right wing was composed of Colonel Levier's regiment, and Major Winston's and McDowell's battalions commanded by Levier himself; the left wing was composed of Colonel Cleveland's regiment, the followers of Colonels Williams, Lacy, Hawthorne, and Hill, headed by Colonel Cleveland in person. In this order the mountaineers pursued until they found Ferguson securely encamped on King's Mountain, which was about half a mile long, and from which he declared the evening before, that "God Almighty" could not drive him. On approaching the mountain, the two centre columns deployed to the right and left, formed a front, and attacked the enemy, while the right and left wings were marching to surround him. In a few minutes the action became general and severe, — continuing furiously for three-fourths of an hour, — when the enemy, being driven from the east to the west end of the mountain, surrendered at discretion. Ferguson was killed, with three hundred and seventy-five of his officers and men, and seven hundred and thirty captured. The Americans had sixty killed and wounded; of the former, Colonel Williams. This glorious achievement occurred at the most gloomy period of the Revolution, and was the first link in the great chain of events to the South which established the independence of the United States. History has heretofore, though improperly, ascribed this merit to the battle of the Cowpens, in January, 1781 ; but it belongs, justly, to the victory on King's Mountain, which turned the tide of war to the South, as the victory of Trenton under Washington, and of Bennington under Stark, did to the North. It was achieved by raw, undisciplined riflemen, without any authority from the government under which they lived; without pay, rations, ammunition, or even the expectation of reward, other than that which results from the noble ambition of advancing the liberty and welfare of their beloved country. It completely dispirited the Tories, and so alarmed Cornwallis, who then lay only thirty miles north of King's Mountain with the main British army, that, on securing information of Ferguson's total defeat and overthrow by the riflemen of the West, under Colonels Campbell, Shelby, Cleveland, and Levier, and that they were bearing down upon him, he ordered an immediate retreat; marched all night in the utmost confusion, and retrograded as far back as Trainsborough, sixty or eighty miles, whence he did not attempt to advance until reinforced three months after by General Leslie, with two thousand men from the Chesapeake. In the mean time the militia of North Carolina assembled in considerable force at New Providence, on the border of South Carolina, under General Davidson; and General Smallwood, with Morgan's light corps and the Maryland line, advanced to the same point. General Gates, with the shattered remains of his army collected at Hillsborough, also came. up, as well as the new levies from Virginia, of one thousand men, under General Stevens. This force enabled General Green, who assumed the command early in December, to hold Cornwallis in check.

The Legislature of North Carolina passed a vote of thanks to Colonel Shelby and several other officers, and directed each to be presented with an elegant sword for their patriotic conduct in the attacks and defeat of the enemy on King's Mountain, on the memorable 7th of October, 1780. This resolution was carried into effect as to Colonel Shelby, in the summer of 1813, just at the moment when, in the language of Secretary Monroe, "disclaiming all metaphysical distinctions tending to enfeeble the Government," he was about to lead his troops far beyond the limits of the State of which he was Governor. The presentation, at that particular time, afforded a presage of the new glory he was to acquire for himself and country in that eventful campaign. If any were entitled to special commendation in this band of heroic spirits on King's Mountain, the claim of Colonel Shelby would be well founded. He originated the expedition, and his valor and unshaken resolution contributed to rally the right of the front line, when driven down the mountain by a tremendous charge from the enemy at the outset of the battle. Nor have the histories of the war in the South done justice to the sagacity and judgment of Colonel Shelby upon another interesting occasion just following the affair on King's Mountain. As soon as he had placed the prisoners beyond the reach of the enemy, he repaired to the headquarters of General Gates, and suggested to him the plan of detaching General Morgan towards the mountains. The details of this arrangement were submitted by him, and approved by Gates, and Greene had the good sense to adopt them, after he assembled the command. The result of his advice was exhibited in the splendid affair at the Cowpens, which added fresh laurels to the veteran brows of *Morgan, Howard*, and *Washington.*

In the campaign of the fall of 1781, Colonel Shelby served under General Marion, a distinguished partisan officer of the boldest enterprise. He was called down by General Greene to that lower country, with five hundred mounted riflemen from the Western waters, in September, 1781, to aid the General in intercepting Cornwallis, at that time blockaded by the French fleet in the Chesapeake, and who, it was suspected, would endeavor to make good his retreat through North Carolina to Charleston; but, upon his lordship's surrender in Virginia, Colonel Shelby was attached to General Marion's command below, on the Santee, and was second in command of a strong detachment of dragoons under Colonel Mayhew, ordered to carry a British post at Fairlawn, near Monk's Corner, eight or ten miles below the enemy's main army under General

Stuart. Information had been received by General Marion that five hundred Hessians, at that post, were in a state of mutiny, and would surrender to any considerable force that might appear before it. But the officer commanding the post, having some apprehensions of their fidelity, had marched them off to Charleston the day before Colonel Mayhew appeared before it. The post, however, was surrendered with one hundred and fifty British prisoners. The British General at Ferguson's Swamp, nine miles in the rear, made great, though unavailing efforts to intercept Mayhew's party on their return with their prisoners to General Marion's encampment. Immediately after this excursion, the British commander retreated with his whole force to Charleston.

As the period for which the mounted volunteers had engaged to serve was about to expire, and no further active operations being contemplated after the retreat of the enemy towards Charleston, Colonel Shelby obtained leave of absence from General Marion to attend the Assembly of North Carolina (of which he was a member), which would sit two hundred miles distant, about the first of December. Marion addressed a letter on the subject to General Greene, which Colonel Shelby was permitted to see, speaking in high terms of the conduct of the mountaineers, and assigning particular credit to Colonel Shelby for his conduct in the capture of the British post, as it surrendered to him after an ineffectual attempt by an officer of the dragoons.

In 1782 Colonel Shelby was elected a member of the North Carolina Assembly, and was appointed one of the commissioners to settle the preëmption claims upon the Cumberland river, and to lay off the lands allotted to the officers and soldiers of the North Carolina line, south of where Nashville now stands. He performed this service in the winter of 1782-83, and returned to Boonsborough, Ky., in April following, where he married Susanna, second daughter of Captain Nathaniel Hart, one of the first

settlers of Kentucky, and one of the proprietors styled
Henderson & Co., by their purchase of the county from the
Cherokees.

He established himself on the first settlement and pre-
emption granted in Kentucky, for the purpose of pursuing
his favorite occupation, the cultivation of the soil; and it
is a remarkable fact, pregnant with many curious reflections,
that, at the period of his death, forty-three years after, he
was the only individual in the State residing upon his
own settlement and preëmption. He was a member of
the early conventions held at Danville for the purpose of
obtaining a separation from the State of Virginia; and
was' a member of that convention which formed the first
constitution of Kentucky in April, 1792. In May following
he was elected the first chief magistrate, and discharged its
arduous duties with signal advantage to the State. The
history of his administration of an infant republic in the
remote wilderness would fill a volume with deeply inter-
'esting incidents, exhibiting him advantageously in the
character of a soldier, of a lawgiver, and a diplomatist;
but the limits prescribed to this sketch will not permit a
detail of them.

After completing the organization of the government
under the constitution by filling the various offices created
by it, the earnest attention of the Governor was directed to
the defence of the State against the Indian incursions and
the border war to which the people were exposed by their
remote and unprotected position in the wilderness. General Washington's paternal regard to the same high object
was manifested in the cautious and extensive arrangements
which were made under the direction of General Wayne
for a strong expedition against the Northwestern Indians
who were stimulated and aided by the British and provincial forces occupying posts within our boundary. The
confidence of Washington, as well as of the people of
Kentucky, was reposed in the energy and patriotism of
Governor Shelby. This was evinced in his almost unan-

imous election to the chief magistracy, as well as in the answer of the first legislature to his message, and in a letter from General Knox, Secretary of War, of July 12, 1792.

In the subsequent letter from the War Department, the defensive operations for the protection of Kentucky were committed exclusively to his judgment and discretion ; and, whenever there was a prospect of acting offensively against the Indians of the Northwest, the President made an appeal to his patriotism and that of the State in furnishing mounted volunteers in aid of the regular force. His energy and the gallantry of Kentucky was signally displayed in the valuable succor rendered to General Wayne on the memorable 20th of August, 1794. His enlightened forecast and the valor of Kentucky contributed on this occasion, as on the equally glorious 5th of October, 1813, the means of victory both in men and transportation, at a critical moment leading to victories more decisive in their results than any heretofore proven in Indian warfare.

While the people of Kentucky were interrupted in their business and prosperity by the attention necessary to the progress of the Indian war, they were annoyed by continued apprehensions of losing the navigation of the Mississippi on which their commercial existence depended. In the midst of these difficulties, a new and unexpected occasion presented itself for the display of Governor Shelby's diplomatic sagacity. The complaints and remonstrances of the Spanish minister induced the general government to open a correspondence with Governor Shelby, for the purpose of suppressing an expedition, which was represented to be in contemplation by La Chaise and other French agents against the possessions of Spain on the Mississippi. Governor Shelby had no apprehensions that they would succeed in organizing the necessary force, and under this impression his reply to the Department of State, October 5th, 1793, was forwarded without considering that he had not authority under existing laws to interfere in preventing it. But the granting of commissions to General Clarke and other influential individuals, and the actual attempt to carry the plans of French emissaries into effect, induced the Governor to examine the subject more thoroughly; and, conceiving that he had no legal authority to interfere, he addressed a letter, January 13th, 1794, to the Secretary of State, expressing these doubts, and assuming an attitude which, though professing the most devoted regard to the Union, had the effect of drawing from the general Government a full development of the measures which had been pursued for securing the navigation of the Mississippi. These explanations by the Department of State and by the special commissioner, the eloquent Colonel James Innes, Attorney-General of Virginia, who was deputed by General Washington to proceed to Kentucky, to communicate with the Governor and Legislature, removed all ground for uneasiness, and created a tranquillity in the public mind which had not existed since the first settlement of the State.

The whole subject was communicated by Governor Shelby to the Legislature on the 15th of November, 1794; and the part he took in it was approved by that body. The act of Congress, on the subject, passed after the receipt of Governor Shelby's letter, shows conclusively that the legislature of the United States did not conceive that previously he had authority to interfere in the mode recommended by the Department of State. This measure on the part of Governor Shelby, though it might seem to conflict with the opinions and policy of General Washington, did not produce in the mind of the father of his country any diminution of the respect and confidence he had theretofore reposed in him; for, in May following, General Knox, Secretary of War, in a letter detailing the plans of the general government in relation to Wayne's proposed campaign, takes occasion to say that "the President, confiding in the patriotism and good disposition of your Excellency, requests that you will afford all the facilities, countenance, and aid in your power, to the proposed expe-

22

dition; and from which, if successful, the State of Kentucky will reap the most abundant advantages." In the
next paragraph he is appointed president of the Board for
selecting the field and company officers, and concludes
with the assurance that General Wayne has been written
to not to interfere in the defensive protection of Kentucky,
which is hereby, in the name of the President of the United
States, confided to your Excellency under the following
general paragraph, &c., &c.

At the close of his gubernatorial term, he returned to his
farm, in Lincoln, with renewed relish for the cares and
enjoyments which its management necessarily created. He
was as distinguished for the method, and judgment, and
industry, which he displayed in agricultural pursuits, as he
had exemplified in the more conspicuous duties of the
general and statesman. He was the model of an elevated
citizen, whether at the plough, in the field, or in the cabinet.

He was repeatedly chosen an elector of President, and
voted for Mr. Jefferson and Mr. Madison. He could not
yield to the repeated solicitations of influential individuals
in different parts of the State, requesting him to consent to
be a candidate for the chief magistracy, until the exigencies
of our national affairs had brought about a crisis which demanded the services of every patriot. In this contingency
he was elected, upon terms very gratifying to his feelings,
a second time to the chief magistracy at the commencement
of the war, in 1812, with Great Britain. Of his career at
that eventful period it would be impracticable, in the limits
of this sketch, to present even an outline.

His energy, associated with a recollection of his revolutionary fame, aroused the patriotism of the State. In every
direction he developed her resources, and aided in sending
men and supplies to the support of the Northwestern army
under General Harrison. The Legislature of Kentucky, in
the winter of 1812–1813, contemplating the necessity of
some vigorous effort in the course of that year, to regain
the ground lost by the disasters at Detroit and at the River

Raisin, passed a resolution authorizing and requesting the Governor to assume the personal direction of the troops of the State, whenever in his judgment such a step would be necessary. Under this authority, and at the solicitation of General Harrison, he invited his countrymen to meet him at New Port, and accompany him to the scene of active, and, as he predicted, of decisive operations. Upon his own responsibility he authorized the troops to meet him with their horses. Four thousand men rallied to his standard in less than thirty days; and this volunteer force reached the shore of Lake Erie just in time to enable the commander-in-chief to profit by the splendid victory achieved by the genius and heroism of Perry and his associates.

It was a most interesting incident, which augured favorably for the issue of the campaign, that Governor Shelby should arrive at the camp of General Harrison, precisely at the moment when Commodore Perry was disembarking his prisoners. The feelings of congratulation which were exchanged by the three heroes, at the tent of the General on the shore of Lake Erie, may be more readily conceived than described. The writer of this article had been previously dispatched by General Harrison to Commodore Perry, to ascertain the result of the naval battle, and, returning with Perry, was present at this interview.

In the organization which Governor Shelby made of his forces, he availed himself of the character and respectability of the materials at his command.

Generals Henry and Desha were assigned to the command of the two divisions, and General Calmes, Caldwell, King, Chiles, and Calloway to the brigades. His confidential staff was composed, among other respectable citizens, of the names of Adair, Crittenden, and Barry, so well known in the history of the State and of the nation. As Governor of Kentucky, his authority ceased as soon as he passed the limits of the State; but the confidence of General Harrison and of all the troops in his judgment and patriotism was

so exalted, that he was regarded as the mentor of the
campaign, and recognized as the senior major-general of
the Kentucky troops. In the general order of march and
of battle, the post assigned to him was the most important,
and the subsequent battle evinced that the arrangement
was as creditable to the sagacity of General Harrison as it
was complimentary to the valor of Governor Shelby.

In all the movements of the campaign, whether in council
or execution, monuments of his valor and of his energetic
character were erected by the gratitude of the commander-
in-chief, of all his troops, and of the President of the nation,
who spoke officially of his services with the veneration
which belongs only to public benefactors. The Legislature
of Kentucky and the Congress of the United States expressed their sense of his gallant conduct in resolutions
which will transmit his name to posterity as a patriot without reproach, and a soldier without ambition.

The vote of Congress, assigning to him and to General
Harrison each a gold medal commemorative of the decisive
victory on the Thames, was delayed one session in consequence of some prejudice prevailing in the public mind
in relation to General Harrison. As soon as Governor
Shelby was advised of this fact, he solicited his friends in
Congress, through Mr. Clay, *to permit no expression of
thanks to him, unless associated with the name of General
Harrison.* This magnanimous conduct and the unqualified
commendation which he gave of the career of General
Harrison on that campaign, connected with a favorable
report of a committee at the next session of Congress,
instituted at the request of the General, of which Colonel
R. M. Johnson was chairman, led to the immediate adoption of the original resolution.

Governor Shelby was unremitting in the aid which he
extended to the operations of the general government
during the war. He furnished troops to defend the country
around Detroit, and dispatched an important reinforcement
to General Jackson for the defence of New Orleans. His

sagacity led him to send General Adair, as adjutant-general
with the rank of brigadier-general, to meet the precise
contingency, which actually occurred, of General Thomas
being sick or disabled.   The result of this measure was exhibited in the critical succor afforded by General Adair on
the memorable 8th of January.   In the civil administration
of the State, Governor Shelby's policy continued to establish and confirm the sound principles of his predecessors.
Integrity, fidelity to the Constitution, and capacity; were
the qualifications which he required in public officers ; and
his recommendations in the Legislature enforced a strict
regard to public economy and to the claims of public faith.
In, the fall of 1816 his term expired, and he retired again to
the sweets of domestic life, in the prosecution of his favorite
pursuit.

In March, 1817, he was selected by President Monroe
to fill the Department of War ; but his advanced age, the
details of the office, and his desire in a period of peace to
remain in private life, induced him to decline an acceptance
of it.   In 1818, he was commissioned by the President to
act, in conjunction with General Jackson, in forming a treaty
with the Chickasaw tribe of Indians, for the purchase of
their lands west of Tennessee river within the limits of
Kentucky and Tennessee, and they obtained a cession of
the territory of the United States, which unites the Western
population, and adds greatly to the defence of the country
in the event of future wars with the savages or with any
European power.   This was his last public act.

In February, 1820, he was attacked with a paralytic
affection, which disabled his right arm, and which was the
occasion of his walking lame on the right leg.   His mind
continued unimpaired until his death by apoplexy on the
18th July, 1826, in the seventy-sixth year of his age.   It
was a consolation to his afflicted family to cherish the
hope that he was prepared for this event.   In the vigor of
life he professed it to be his duty to dedicate himself to
God, and to seek an interest in the merits of the Redeemer.

He had been for many years a member of the Presbyterian
Church; and in his latter days he was the chief instrument in erecting a house of worship upon his own land.
The vigor of his constitution fitted him to endure active
and severe bodily exercise, and the energetic symmetry of
his person, united with a peculiar suavity of manner, ren--
dered his deportment impressively dignified; his strong,
natural sense was aided by close observation on men and
things; and the valuable qualities of method and perseverance imparted success to all his efforts.

STUDIES IN LITERATURE.

By G. W. GRIFFIN,

UNITED STATES CONSUL AT COPENHAGEN.

New Revised Edition.

12mo. $1.75.

CLAXTON, REMSEN & HAFFELFINGER,

PHILADELPHIA.

From the Philadelphia Age.

The volume opens with a portraiture of George D. Prentice, the widely known editor of the Louisville "Journal." The author was his personal friend. The insight which it gives into the character of Mr. Prentice, will interest all who have heard of his prose and poetry. Besides a number of careful and very original criticisms on the Plays of Shakspeare, we find two articles on Booth's Hamlet and Macbeth. Our national pride in the fame of this dramatic artist is a warrant that these notices of him will be read, and they will be found to contain the best elements of criticism, intelligence, and good taste.

From the Philadelphia Press.

Varied in its range of subject, rich in thought, light and graceful in treatment and style, and the result of wide and conscientious study, we can commend this volume unhesitatingly as an admirable selection for general reading. Æsthetically, its educational influence will be most happy.

From the New York Home Journal.

Mr. Griffin treats, in the present volume, twenty-two subjects with wonderful originality and clearness. Poets, actors, dramatists, and philologists whose names are familiar to the educated of both hemispheres, are sketched with rare skill; and one lingers over his descriptions, and his chaste, beautiful English, with no ordinary pleasure.

From the Cincinnati Enquirer.

The best notice we have ever seen of Mr. Prentice and his works, is from the pen of Mr. Griffin — the first of a series of biographical sketches in this volume. It is characterized, as all his articles are, by historical and literary research, by great purity of diction and vigor of style.

From the New Orleans Times.

A new edition of a work very favorably received upon its first publication. It consists of a series of essays upon prominent topics, including some excellent theatrical reviews, written in chaste style, and with considerable power.   The work will commend itself to all   1

From the Carlisle Mercury.
It is, indeed, as is indicated by its title, a study in literature, and should be in the hands of every intelligent person.

From R. Shelton Mackenzie.
The recollections of the late Geo. D. Prentice, the great newspaper editor, are so considerably extended as indeed to form a satisfactory biography. Mr. Griffin handles his subject with delicacy and vigor; he doth " nothing extenuate," but presents a true portrait of one who was very eminent in his profession, who might (and ought to)have stood in the van of American literati, but who, in newspaper work, on which his life was spent —

" To party gave up what was meant for mankind."

Through Mr. Griffin, in this sketch, a very intimate knowledge of Prentice and his varying moods of mind can be formed. Not alone his readiness and wit, but the tenderness and poetry of his nature are brought before the reader. Considering how fugitive is the fame of even the greatest of the journalistic craft, very fortunate has George D. Prentice been in having such a permanent memorial from the friendship, the ability, and the judgment of Mr. Griffin.

From Paul R. Shipman.
This interesting volume deserves all the praise it has received. It is characterized by deep thought, careful research, mature judgment, and rhetorical grace of very high order. Mr. Griffin calls his essays studies. If they are studies, what may we *not* expect from his mature performances! The world, I predict, will not have to wait long to see.

From Henry T. Stanton.
The first pages in this valuable book are devoted to a sketch of the life and character of Mr. Prentice, and a highly interesting account of his death. We have never read a more impressive article. While it contains every elegance requisite to finished writing, it is full of that irrepressible feeling, that genuine warmth of attachment, for which mere words are no medium of expression. The author has put his heart in his labor, and all his essays appear inspired.

From the Louisville Courier Journal.
Next to a good hater, we like an ardent lover. No one can read the sketch of Geo. D. Prentice's life in the revised and enlarged edition of Mr. Griffin's Studies in Literature, without being impressed by the warm and enthusiastic tribute to that remarkable editor and man of letters. It is the eulogy of a friend who can only speak of what was noble and wise.   2

Mr. Griffin is an easy writer. Some of his criticisms and general essays indicate the faithful and studious course of reading pursued. His essay on Vathek and its author details many interesting points not known to the general reader. A Philological Study contains much useful information. The examples taken in illustration, prove to what an extent the English language is misused.

Mr. Griffin is a conscientious and painstaking writer. The intimacy which existed between him and the great statesman, journalist, and phi-. losopher Prentice, was one of the most cordial character, and the writer of this note can vouch for the fidelity with which Mr. Griffin has told the story of the great man's life, and presented to the reader a pen-picture of the closing scene of a great career.

The new revised edition of G. W. Griffin's Studies in Literature has been accepted as a text-book by the faculty of " Forest Academy," and will hereafter be used as a reading-book for the advanced scholars of this well-known institution of learning.

The most noticeable of these papers, which Mr. Griffin is so kind as to call "studies," is a memoir of the late George D. Prentice, of the Louisville " Journal." In fact, it was the success which this paper met with upon its first publication which has induced the writer to rewrite and enlarge it, and to give it the place of honor in the second edition. The author writes with a gracefulness of diction which is evidently the result of long practice.

"Studies in Literature" consists of a collection of essays on literary, biographical, and dramatic subjects, generally well written, and evidently the work of a refined and cultivated mind.

The very large sale of the first edition of this tasteful, valuable, and substantial contribution to American literature, by a gifted Kentuckian, was not unanticipated by Mr. Griffin's immediate friends, and fully justifies the warm greeting and cordial recognition accorded it by the " Yeoman " upon its first appearance.

The book is the product of careful research and mature thought. It compares most favorably in these respects with the best literature of this country.

3